HER HERO

Boston Doms Book Six

JANE HENRY
MAISY ARCHER

Published by Blushing Books
An Imprint of
ABCD Graphics and Design, Inc.
A Virginia Corporation
977 Seminole Trail #233
Charlottesville, VA 22901

©2017
All rights reserved.

No part of the book may be reproduced or transmitted in any form or by any means, electronic or mechanical, including photocopying, recording, or by any information storage and retrieval system, without permission in writing from the publisher. The trademark Blushing Books is pending in the US Patent and Trademark Office.

Jane Henry and Maisy Archer
Her Hero
v1

EBook ISBN: 978-1-61258-245-0
Print ISBN: 978-1-64563-164-4

Cover Art by ABCD Graphics & Design
This book contains fantasy themes appropriate for mature readers only. Nothing in this book should be interpreted as Blushing Books' or the author's advocating any non-consensual sexual activity.

Chapter 1

Donnie eased his Valkyrie to a smooth stop at a red light on Harbor Road and shifted his head from side to side, trying to ease the tension that always gripped his shoulders after hours spent on his bike.

Christ, what a perfect day. Unseasonably mild for April in New England, it was all warm sunshine and cool breezes that could have tempted even the most devoted workaholic to play hooky. And as much as he loved his job managing The Club South and overseeing the ongoing transformation of the dilapidated old firehouse into the premiere BDSM playhouse south of Boston, Donnie had never claimed to be *that* dedicated. Instead, he'd done what his boss, Master Blake, was always encouraging him to do, and he'd *delegated*, leaving the deliveries, the contractors, and the paperwork in the capable hands of his team while he escaped for the day to clear his head.

Donnie had been up at dawn with his saddlebags packed and his playlist loaded, letting a flip of the coin determine that *north* would be his direction for the day. He'd been on the road early enough to avoid all the rush hour traffic as he'd cruised from

Quincy through Boston, sticking to the highways as far as the Maine border and then detouring for a slow, scenic ride up and down Route 1. Just him, his trusty Valk, and the rocky Atlantic coastline stretching as far as the eye could see. He'd grabbed an early dinner at a seafood shack that was nearly empty of tourists this early in the season, before heading back south. And now, as the last streaks of orange twilight lit the sky, he found himself only two blocks from the place he called home—a room above The Club with a view of the water and the Boston skyline, where a scalding hot shower awaited him. Anticipation and pleasure curled in his gut.

In a life where not a lot had gone *right*, let alone *perfectly*, Donnie Nolan knew better than to take this stuff for granted.

As he straddled the vibrating machine, appreciating the salty tang in the air and the crash of the waves just beyond the sea wall, a flash of light in his side mirror caught his attention. He watched with detached amusement as a giant fucking behemoth of a bike pulled onto the shoulder of the road, passing half a dozen cars, and coming to a stop beside Donnie. It was the kind of illegal, douchebag move that gave bikers everywhere a bad rep. Not content with his Asshole status, the guy then edged his bike forward in impatient bursts that had a mom yanking her toddler back from the crosswalk. He then leveled up to *Fucking Asshole* by revving his engine loud enough for the people standing outside the ice cream shop across the street to crane their heads and look for the source of the noise.

Jesus, what a fuckwit.

Donnie wouldn't turn his head or give the guy the attention he was clearly asking for, but from behind his own full-coverage helmet, he could see that the other man had swiveled to look at him. Dude had long white hair tied back in a long tail, no helmet on his head, and a taunting smile on his face that got Donnie's back up.

And that was before he started mouthing obscenities.

The guy was looking for trouble. A race? A fight? Who the fuck knew? And he was trying to goad Donnie into joining him. And for the briefest of seconds, Donnie almost allowed himself to be persuaded. He could imagine swinging his leg over his bike, throwing his helmet off, and decking the asshole. Donnie knew exactly how it would feel when the flesh and bone of his knuckles made contact with the other guy's face, how the shock of the blow would reverberate up his arm to his shoulder, how all the rational processes of his brain would short-circuit, and a red haze would descend across his vision. He'd be a warrior once more, the tip of a spear, the chief leg-breaker in Mikey Nolan's personal army, the instinct-driven animal he'd been trained to be. He almost craved the black-and-white simplicity of it. *It's him or me. Gotta fight, gotta win.*

And then the light changed, sanity returned, and Donnie gestured the douchebag ahead with an ironic wave of his gloved hand. *After you, motherfucker.*

As the guy disappeared down the crowded street, weaving around stopped cars, Donnie slowly let out the clutch on his own bike, allowing himself to roll forward. He took a deep breath, forcing down the spike of adrenaline that made him want to chase after the other guy and teach him a lesson.

Not fucking worth it, he reminded himself. *True strength lies in control.*

He'd learned almost half a lifetime ago that when you let someone draw you into a fight, when you let *them* dictate the terms of a confrontation, you *always* lost, even when you won.

The Bluetooth speaker inside his helmet played out the first mournful notes of Lynyrd Skynyrd's *Simple Man*—the ringtone Donnie had assigned to his friend and mentor Blake Coleman. Donnie pushed away the last vestiges of his annoyance as he hit the button on his helmet to accept the call.

"Evening, boss," he spoke into the mic as traffic crept along. He noticed with a smirk that his voice was raspy tonight, gravelly from disuse the way it always got when he'd spent the day alone on the road. Yeah, he'd paid a fair bit for a helmet that he *could* use to make and accept calls, but he could count on two hands the number of people who had his cell number, and even fewer he'd bother to talk to while he was riding. Blake was one of them.

"North or south?" Blake asked without preamble, amusement evident in his deep voice.

Donnie snorted. He hadn't shared his plans with Blake this morning beyond a quick text to say that he'd be out-of-pocket for the day, but it didn't surprise him that Blake already knew. Blake wouldn't waste time asking stupid shit, like "What did you do today?" or "Did you have fun?" because the answers would be, "Riding," and "Fuck, yeah." *Every single time*.

"North," Donnie replied, feeling a weird warmth in his chest that came from having someone know him that well and give a shit about his welfare. It was a feeling he wasn't entirely used to, even after knowing Blake for more than a decade. The only other person who'd ever given him that feeling was Grace, and she was…

God. He hadn't allowed himself to think of Grace in years, hadn't allowed himself to fully conjure her face or imagine what her life might be like these days. But just when he thought he'd succeeded in scrubbing her from his thoughts, locking every cherished memory in a vault, her name would appear right in front of him, taunting him with what could never be.

He swallowed and forced himself to finish the thought. *Grace was ancient history. A closed chapter. Another thing he'd been forced to leave behind.*

"Knew it. Elena owes me," Blake said, with a note of satisfaction in his voice that brought Donnie's attention back to the present. "You headed west last time, and east the time before that. Figured it'd be north or south."

Donnie snorted again. "Uh, boss, you know I toss a coin to decide this shit, right? Not exactly the kind of thing you wanna bet on?"

Blake's chuckle was low and meaningful. "Only if I cared about losing this *particular* bet, Don."

Jesus.

"Right," Donnie said, rolling his eyes as he put on his blinker, pulled into the lot behind the three-story red brick building, and eased into his parking spot.

Given all the years he'd worked for Blake at The Club, first as a bouncer, then a Dungeon Master, and now as a Club manager, Donnie figured he'd seen and done pretty much everything. But somehow even the most vaguely suggestive reference to Blake's much-younger wife Elena, a woman Donnie had come to think of as his adopted older sister, made him squirm and quickly switch the subject.

"So, are we still meeting tomorrow afternoon? Second floor construction is done, but I want to walk you through the third floor before I give the general contractor the final sign-off."

Blake hummed a negative. "Tomorrow's not good. Slay's got shit to do, and I want him and Matt to be there for this meet. *I* was down there a couple weeks ago, but the other guys haven't seen the place since we opened on New Year's Eve."

Alexander Slater and Matteo Angelico, both well-respected

and experienced dominants who had worked with Blake for years, had bought into The Club a few years ago, just before the opening of the third location, The Club North. Though the transition from sole proprietor to partner had been a bit tricky for Blake in the beginning, Donnie personally felt that Blake was happier now that he could devote more time to Elena and their kids.

"I want them to see how much you've accomplished," Blake continued. "You should be proud."

Donnie cleared his throat. He wasn't shy. He knew he'd worked his ass off, and he was confident he'd done a good job, but he had no idea how to handle Blake's praise. He never had.

"No big, boss," he muttered.

"No big?" Blake echoed. "That building was ready to be condemned six months ago, Donnie. And honest to God, for a second there, I wondered if we'd bitten off more than we could chew, but you turned it around. In two months, you had all construction on the first floor completed six weeks ahead of schedule, you had over a hundred members lined up before opening night, and now you have us open four nights a week, when we'd only planned to be open three until mid-summer."

"I had help," Donnie argued, feeling the tension in his neck ratchet up a notch.

"Yup. An almost-entirely new team that *you* hired, vetted, and trained. Your staff is pretty damn impressive too."

Donnie wanted to dispute this, but he was too caught up on Blake's last words.

His staff. God, wasn't *that* a fucking kick? Donnie Nolan, the perpetual fuckup who would've won "Most Likely to Serve Hard Time" if he'd bothered sticking with high school long enough to see his senior year, had big responsibilities these days and a fucking *staff* of men and women who reported to him.

And it was all thanks to the guy on the other end of the phone, who'd somehow seen a spark of potential in a punk-assed, muscle-bound delinquent who was never supposed to amount to anything. Words, never Donnie's strong suit, failed him just then, but he vowed to himself that he'd never give Blake a reason to regret taking a chance on him.

Blake smoothly covered Donnie's lapse. "So, I'm thinking we'll meet the day after tomorrow. Wednesday afternoon or evening. I'll let you know once I confirm with Slay and Matt, yeah?"

"Yeah. Sounds good. See you then," Donnie agreed, before disconnecting the call and finally shutting off his bike.

The sounds of traffic from Harbor Road seemed even louder after Donnie removed his helmet and tucked it under his arm. It was fully dark now, and as he crossed the parking lot and opened the back door, he made a note to himself that they needed to bump up the lighting in this lot ASAP. It was entirely too dark out here for his peace of mind.

He climbed the short flight of stairs to the main floor, where one of the bouncers would normally be stationed on an open night, unzipping his leather riding jacket as he went. Tonight, the lights were low and the rooms on this level—a large bar, a dance floor, and three demonstration rooms—were deserted. All the construction workers had gone home hours ago, and none of the staff were scheduled.

He debated a detour to the stockroom, to make sure Andy had received and organized the liquor delivery properly, but the lure of his own space, the third-floor suite Blake had insisted he remodel before any of the other rooms, was too strong. Shower, hydrate, bed, in that order.

He'd just put his foot on the first step to the second floor when a creak above alerted him that he wasn't alone.

Instinctive caution, born of years spent under the thumbs of first his alcoholic asshole father and then his psycho cousin Mikey, had him looking around for a weapon. He placed his helmet on the table near the main entrance and dipped his hand into his pocket, threading his keys through his fingers. He climbed the stairs quickly and quietly, keeping his feet on the thick carpet runner that ran down the middle of the treads. The Club hadn't had any trouble with security at any of its locations in a long while; not since drug kingpin Chalo Salazar had been given a two-year prison stint and managed to win himself an extra year for bad behavior, and Donnie didn't anticipate any trouble now, but it was always better to be prepared.

"Master Nolan? *Sir*? Is that you?"

The plaintive whine had him stopping in his tracks three steps from the top. *Oh, Christ.* Suddenly, he was almost wishing for one of Salazar's goons to appear.

"Julie. You're here late." He made his voice as distant as possible as he shuffled up the last three steps, dropping his keys back in his pocket.

The petite brunette stood in the middle of the second-floor foyer, biting her bottom lip nervously, her eyes cast to the floor. She wore a short black dress that clung to her curves like a second skin and some strappy, death-defying heels—the kind of thing that the girls normally wore when they were off-duty, and at The Club to play or to participate in a demonstration.

"Yeah. I, um… I just finished up," she said, waving behind

her in the general direction of the office, which was located at the front of the building, directly above the main entrance.

Donnie pursed his lips at this outright lie. Julie was a waitress and bartender who worked (and *played*) almost exclusively downstairs. There was no reason for her to be hanging around the office at all. Still, he hesitated to call her out on it. He was pretty sure her real reason for being there had to do with seeing *him*, and the hopeful glances she was sneaking him from under her lashes only confirmed it.

He'd first noticed a change in her behavior a few weeks back, not long after she'd volunteered to participate in a Shibari demonstration with him. From his perspective, it had been a purely professional thing. Though he'd had to touch her quite a bit as he demonstrated the correct roping and knotting procedures, he'd remained as aloof and clinical as possible; his usual MO during demos. But despite his precautions, she'd somehow gotten the wrong idea. She'd started popping up wherever he was, calling him *Sir* in a breathy voice, and giving him shy smiles that seemed calculated to entice any dominant who was in the market for a long-term submissive.

Unfortunately for her, Donnie was in the market to rent rather than to own. All of his relationships could be better measured in *hours* than in years. But even if he *had* been looking for something more permanent, even if he *weren't* her boss, Julie just wasn't his type.

Donnie frowned and tried to put his finger on what bugged him about the girl. She was pretty enough, for sure, with long brown hair, brown eyes, and the petite, curvy figure he'd always enjoyed on a woman. But there seemed to be something hiding behind her eyes—a sort of calculation, like she was trying to project the image of the type of sub she *thought* he wanted.

Maybe some guys got off on the whole "I'll be whatever you need me to be!" vibe, but Donnie wasn't one of them. *Christ*, if there was one thing that he hated about the BDSM scene these days, it was the drama, the over-the-top fantasy that so many people seemed to be looking for. He knew that *real* dominant/submissive relationships, like the kinds that his friends Matteo, Slay, Dom, Tony, and Paul had with their partners required work and compromise, and he'd seen firsthand what it had taken for Blake and Elena to negotiate their rocky start.

Step one was to be honest with yourself *and* your partner about what you needed. If you weren't ready and willing to do that—and God knew, Donnie wasn't fucking ready to share his deepest, darkest desires with *anyone*—you had no business getting involved in anything complicated.

That was why, if Julie kept up with this shit, Donnie was gonna have to figure out how to say "No fucking way" in a diplomatic manner that spared her feelings, while leaving no doubt that they would never have an association beyond a professional one.

Words, diplomacy, feelings.

Fuck.

He'd rather beat the shit out of something any day.

There had only ever been one woman he could talk to without restraint, without the words getting twisted halfway between his brain and his tongue. Grace.

Jesus, Nolan, he chastised himself. *Resurrecting ghosts twice in one night? Focus.*

"So, um, have you eaten? Dinner, I mean?" Julie asked nervously, when it became clear that Donnie wasn't going to pick up the conversation.

"Yep," he confirmed. "A while ago. I'm getting ready to turn in."

He folded his arms across his chest and waited for her to take the hint.

She didn't.

"Would you maybe want to, you know, *hang out?*" she persisted. "I noticed that you hardly ever stop by the playrooms unless you're giving a demo. We could maybe practice the cane thing you're doing tomorrow night?"

Donnie sighed. No way to avoid it. He ran a hand through his chin-length blond hair and dove in.

"Think you got the wrong idea," he said stiffly. "We ain't gonna hang out. I'm your boss."

"Oh." She blinked. "But, um, is there a rule against employees hanging out? Because I heard through the grapevine that Slay was Alice's manager and they, um… you know."

Donnie suppressed a growl. How much clearer could he be? Yeah, everyone knew the story of how Slay had met and fallen hard for his wife, Allie, back when she'd worked the main bar at The Club, but that didn't fucking matter.

"I'm not Slay," Donnie said flatly. "I don't get involved with my employees."

"Oh," Julie said again. She looked momentarily crestfallen, but then rallied and took a step closer to him. "Because I wouldn't tell anyone…"

"Not the point," he said, his low voice brooking no argument. "I need you to keep your behavior professional, or there will be consequences, up to and including termination."

"T-termination?" she stammered, licking her lips nervously. "No! I can do professional. I, uh… I understand. I love this job. I *need* this job, Master Nolan."

Donnie nodded and felt a faint stirring of pity. He knew what *that* felt like.

"Good," he told her. "I'm relieved to hear that." And then, something compelled him to add, "Listen, Julie, lots of the girls here, and at The Club Boston seem… nice. Friendly. If you need someone to talk to…"

Julie bit her lip and Donnie trailed off as someone started pounding on the door below.

What now?

He saw Julie's eyes flash in surprise, and as he hurried down the stairs, she followed.

The banging had increased in volume and tempo by the time he made it to the first floor, and was accompanied by a man shouting in garbled English.

"Don! Open up, man! Oh, *fuck*, Donnie! Open the damn door!"

"Stand back," he clipped at Julie, who nodded with wide eyes before moving around the corner into one of the demo rooms.

Once she was out of sight, Donnie unlocked the door and threw it open… only to have the guy who'd been shouting fall directly at Donnie's feet.

The man pushed himself to his hands and knees on the hardwood floor and glanced up. Donnie automatically stepped back into a defensive position, reaching for the stupid keys in his pocket and wishing, not for the first time, that he hadn't stopped carrying his Glock when he'd left his cousin's employ. The dude's face was a bloody mess. His nose was unmistakably broken, his mouth distorted, one dark eye swollen shut, and his clothes, which seemed to have started out as a high-end suit and silk shirt, were shredded, not like they'd been ripped or worn out, but…

Oh, motherfucker.

Sliced.

The man had been beaten and sliced, right through the fabric of his clothing, into his skin in dozens and dozens of places all over his body. With no more than a cursory glance, Donnie knew they were shallow wounds—bruises delivered by hand and cuts from a straight razor, precisely calibrated to scare, to scar, to *hurt*, but not to kill. And he knew, just as well as he knew the brown eyes he saw in the mirror each morning, that this poor fuck-up had been forced to count the strikes himself while a bunch of neighborhood punks who desperately wanted to be badasses had held him down by his hands and ankles. There would be one blow or cut for each thousand the guy owed. A gruesome, permanent accounting of his debt because that was the kind of twisted justice that Mikey Nolan found amusing.

Donnie ground his teeth together. His cousin had worked this guy over thoroughly, and Donnie couldn't help but feel bad for the sap. But it had been years—*God*, more than a decade—since he'd had anything to do with Mikey's shit. So why the fuck was this guy here? And how did he know Donnie's name?

Donnie felt a sense of foreboding settle in his gut.

"Donnie," the man pleaded, tears and blood making tracks across his skin. "Help me!"

Donnie narrowed his eyes and looked closer, beyond the bloody wreckage of his face, trying to place the connection. There was something… But it wasn't until the man let his head fall forward with a sob, until a thick hank of dark brown hair fell across his forehead and obscured his swollen eye, that Donnie felt the flare of recognition. He knew that hair. He remembered eyes just like that…

"Christ. Pedro? Is that you?"

. . .

"*Caillate, Gracia Maria!* *You're not coming with us. Not today. And stop whining.*" *Donnie's best friend propped his foot on the built-in seat of the scarred wooden picnic table and combed his fingers carefully through his mop of brown hair, his eyes trained on his reflection in the darkened window of Sully's Grab 'n Go next door.*

"*But why?*" *A little girl, whose dark, serious brown eyes took up nearly half her face, perched on the edge of the wooden table top, her short legs kicking back and forth. In truth, the girl never whined, but she also never gave in without a good reason. A fact which drove her brother crazy but made Donnie laugh.*

"*Because you're too little,* mija.*"*

"*Little! I'm eleven! And I can help. I can carry things. I notice things! It's not fair you guys get go places and have fun without me.*"

"*Donnie and I* are *seventeen. We're men now. We're gonna be working for Mikey, for God's sake. You've gotta stop following us around like a puppy. It's weird.*"

The impatient, superior big-brother tone made Grace's eyes narrow, and Donnie stepped in as he always did, pushing himself out of his slouch against the building and searching for the words that would make her understand.

"*Gracie, there are different ways to be helpful. The place we're going today, the guys we're gonna meet… it might be dangerous.*"

The full force of those shining eyes—eyes glowing with hero worship, and more excited than anxious at the prospect of adventure—swung toward him, and he found himself momentarily stunned. All he could think was, "Holy shit. Someday she's gonna fucking OWN a man with those eyes. She'll break hearts." And he'd felt a quick, confusing clench of anger in his gut at the prospect of Grace ever bestowing that look on anyone but him.

"*So what if it is?*" *Grace challenged.* "*You'll protect me. You said you'd* always *protect me.*"

Donnie nodded, because yeah, of course he would.

"But that's why you can't be there. The two of us would be distracted, worrying about you."

He could see the lightning-quick calculation behind those eyes, and knew she'd reached the right conclusion when her shoulders slumped in defeat.

"When you give an intelligent explanation like that, I can't really argue," she sighed.

Intelligent explanation? Him? A weird, warm feeling curled in his chest, and Donnie absently tried to rub it away.

His friend hooted. "Right, Don's Mr. Intelligent. So smart he didn't need school no more."

Donnie flipped him off behind the girl's back.

"Maybe while we're gone you could work on your drawing? I keep asking you to do a sketch of me," Donnie teased her.

Her cheeks flooded with color and she shook her head. "No way."

Her brother snorted, not looking away from his reflection. "Oh, bro, consider yourself lucky. She sucks. She did a picture of me the other night. Made me look like a fucking donkey, with this big, stupid smile."

Grace's eyes met Donnie's, and she grinned. Donnie didn't know shit about art, but he knew enough about Grace's talent to be sure that if she'd drawn her brother like that, it was totally intentional. Donnie smirked.

"Time to get back inside the house, Gracia," her brother said, turning away from the window. "We've gotta go, and if Papa catches you out here alone…"

Donnie frowned. They were in the Diaz family's own backyard, but even so, Grace wasn't supposed to be outside unsupervised. The nuns at St. Bridget's had fewer rules and restrictions than Mr. Diaz did for his only daughter.

Grace sighed and jumped down from the table, looking so lonely and dejected that Donnie jammed his hands in his pockets and looked away before he did something stupid, like try to give the kid a hug.

But Grace had never let him off the hook that easily. She threw her arms around his waist and squeezed, pressing her cheek against his chest for the *briefest of moments. The smell of her—the faint tang of cinnamon chewing gum that he always associated with his Grace—filled his nose.*

"Come back safe, okay, Donnie?" she asked, turning those bright, solemn eyes up at him, and he was helpless to do anything but nod. Then, after a quick glance at her impatient brother, she turned back to Donnie, rolling her eyes as she pulled away. "And take care of Pedro."

He'd pictured Pedro the way he'd always looked—perfectly mussed hair, round-cheeked baby face, laughing brown eyes, as tall and wiry as Donnie had been at eighteen. But in the intervening years, Donnie had grown, gaining several inches in height and at least forty pounds of solid muscle. Whereas Pedro, Donnie saw, as he helped the man unsteadily to his feet, seemed to have shrunk. He was skin and bones beneath his fine clothing, his shoulders were stooped, and he flinched when Donnie wrapped an arm around his waist and guided him into the bar area.

Donnie hadn't seen Pedro Diaz in nearly a dozen years. Last Donnie had heard, Pedro had been middle management in Mikey's "organization," which was the highest rank Pedro was ever likely to attain, given that he wasn't blood family. He'd assumed the guy was doing well—as well as a man who'd chosen to sell his soul *could* be—but even though Donnie lived minutes away from the old neighborhood, he'd made a point never to go back and check on them. He'd only set foot there once in the past decade. That was Mikey's neighborhood, and always had been. It was safer for everyone who lived there if they weren't associated with Donnie, the cousin who'd disgraced the family by walking away, and it was crucial to Donnie's survival to forget they existed.

Didn't mean Donnie hadn't thought about his friends over

the years, though. He'd imagined P getting married, maybe to one of Donnie's own cousins. More than once, he'd forced himself to confront the fact that Grace was likely married now too, and he hoped the lucky fucker deserved her. He'd read in the paper that Mr. Diaz had died a few years back, and he'd grieved for Pedro and Grace. And right now, as he looked at the pathetic battered man, he could hear the echo of Grace's voice in his head, telling him to take care of Pedro. So, whatever bullshit Pedro was involved in, however he'd incurred Mikey's wrath, Donnie couldn't bring himself to turn his former friend away.

"Sit here," he said, heaving Pedro onto one of the wooden barstools. "Calm yourself. What do you need, man? Hospital?"

"No!" Pedro gasped, leaning heavily against the bar. "No hospital. No cops."

Donnie nodded, not surprised. He ducked beneath the passthrough, collecting ice in a clean towel and opening the first aid kit they always kept on hand beneath the bar, before turning to assess the damage.

The lacerations on Pedro's body would heal with time and some antibiotic goop. Ice would help control the swelling on his face, and it didn't look like he needed stitches. The greatest threat to his health right now was in failing to pay back whatever debt he'd managed to accrue.

"Here," Donnie said, holding out the makeshift ice pack, while he wet a second towel under the tap.

Pedro took the ice and gingerly held it to his swollen eye. "Don, I need your help," he said, attempting to draw a deep breath against ribs that were probably bruised, trying to control the tears streaming down his broken face.

"Yeah. So you said," Donnie agreed, cutting under the passthrough once more. "But, bro, if you managed to cross Mikey somehow… I don't know how you think I can help you."

He approached the other man and braced one hand against his back while grasping his nose with the other. He waited until Pedro gave the barest nod of assent, then set Pedro's broken nose back into place with one deft movement and secured it with strips of sterile tape from the kit.

Pedro barely flinched. "Still got the touch with that, huh? Must be, what, the *third* time you've done that for me?" he asked, his voice thick with pain.

Donnie nodded. "Don't get much practice anymore," he said. And he hadn't missed it.

He wiped his hands off on the towel and took the stool next to Pedro before continuing.

"You know better than anyone that I dragged myself out of Mikey's shit, kicking and screaming. If I get involved again, it'll be a death sentence. We've been through a lot, man, so if you need a place to spend a couple nights, you've got it. And if you need some cash—and by that I mean a couple of thousand, enough to get you out of town, not enough for… *this*," he looked pointedly at the dozens of small cuts up and down Pedro's torso, which had to sting like a sonofabitch. "I'll get it for you. But, P…" He deliberately let his voice go lower, firmer, so there would be no confusion on this score. "There is not a single thing in Heaven or on Earth that will get me involved with Mikey again."

Pedro's eyes, stark with shock and misery, met his.

"They've got Grace, man. They're holding her… until I pay my debts."

And Donnie's world turned red.

"Pick up, pick up, pick up," Donnie muttered, as the phone rang inside his helmet. He was weaving the Valkyrie through the light city traffic in a remarkable impression of the douchebag on the Harley from earlier, and he couldn't care less. He'd been hyper-focused since the moment P had spoken his sister's name, and not a fucking thing existed but Grace and his need to get to her.

Now.

He'd barked orders like a sergeant, clearing away obstacles. He'd called in a favor from Lucas, a guy who worked with Slay, doing what they called "off-the-books security jobs," which seemed to run the gamut from global terrorism prevention to rescuing kittens from trees, and had found someone who could patch Pedro up and give him a place to crash until he'd healed. He'd gotten Julie, who had still been cowering in the demonstration room, out to her fucking car, and out of his hair. And he'd grabbed the wickedly sharp Ka-Bar knife from the box on the top shelf of his closet just in case. Its weight against his thigh felt comforting.

The one obstacle he hadn't been able to surmount was finding out where Grace was being held… and how the hell he'd get her back.

"I fucked up, Donnie," Pedro had admitted. "Moving money, making book, it got old. And I got greedy. I wanted to grab some money—enough to last me a good, long while—and get the fuck out. New guy started cutting into our territory, a young kid named Javi. I never got a handle on who he was working for, but shit started getting chaotic. I thought I could take advantage of it. I lied and told Mikey that Javi had stolen our money…but Mikey found out. I gave him back the money I stole, every penny of the 750 large. But he says he wants me to pay him back *double*, to atone for my sins or… forfeit Grace."

Typical Mikey, handing out penance, knowing full well that there was no way for a man like Pedro to come up with three-quarters of a million dollars.

"How's Grace gonna get him the money?" Donnie had asked.

Pedro had looked at him in disbelief, as if shocked that Donnie was so far gone from his years in Mikey's shit that he couldn't figure it out for himself.

And then he had, and his blood had grown cold. "Sex?"

Pedro had nodded. "Far as I know, Grace's still a virgin, Don. I don't know if she's saving herself for marriage to Prince Charming, or if she just drank too much of the good-girl Kool-Aid that my dad passed out, but I've never seen her with a guy. She's never even dated. And if Mikey has his way, her first time is gonna be sold to the highest bidder and broadcast online."

Over Donnie's dead body.

The ringing in his headset finally stopped and a slurred voice answered. "H'lo?"

"Joe."

Just one word, just the man's name, but it was enough to get his older brother from happy drunk to *allll* worked up.

"I can't talk to you! What the fuck are you doing calling me, Donnie? You're dead to us, remember. Jesus, I have *kids*."

Funny how Donnie had been very much *alive* last year, when Joe's son Declan had been diagnosed with a rare form of cancer and needed a bone marrow donor, wasn't it?

"I'm coming to the house," he said simply.

"No, Don! Fuck. Just... *No*. Meet me somewhere else," his brother begged. "A bar... or..."

"Better open the door," Donnie said. "The longer I stand outside banging, the more the neighbors are gonna get an eyeful.

And we wouldn't want them to get the wrong impression, would we, Joey?"

"You're killin' me, man," Joe whined.

Donnie snorted and disengaged the call. Killing his brother was just the beginning. If those assholes harmed Grace, no one would be safe.

When he arrived at his brother's house a few minutes later, he pulled his bike around to the back, near the rickety old garage, and left his helmet on the seat. He climbed the rear steps two at a time, and the back door opened before he could knock.

"Get in here!" Joe told him, pulling Donnie into the kitchen and making sure none of the neighbors had seen. "Christ, you have no idea, Don…"

His brother was tall and whip-thin, with thinning, sandy hair that had once been bright red. There had been a time, when Don was a kid, that he'd thought Joe was the bravest of the brave, always looking out for Donnie, protecting him from the worst of his father's booze-soaked beatings.

Now, Joe's hands shook with fear.

"Let's get this over with," Donnie said without preamble. "Mikey took Grace Diaz to pay Pedro's debt."

Joe didn't look surprised, but somehow he seemed to grow even more nervous.

"What do you know about that, Joe?" Donnie asked.

Joe licked his lips, but instead of answering, he turned pleading eyes to Don. "Why'd you have to get involved now, Donnie? You haven't been back to this neighborhood in years. Why *now*, huh? Why not just… stay gone?"

A fair question. He hadn't seen Grace Diaz in nearly twelve years; not since he'd been nineteen and she'd been a wide-eyed thirteen-year-old. For all he knew, he'd passed her a hundred times at the grocery store or riding the subway, and hadn't even known. Would he even recognize her as a woman?

It didn't matter, though. Grace was the best part of him—his conscience, his beating heart. The only part of his childhood that he could remember without feeling disgust or shame. Just subconsciously knowing that she was okay, that she still *existed* in the world, had meant that he could keep existing too.

But Joe didn't need to know any of that shit.

"You owe me, Joe."

He hadn't wanted to say those words. You didn't hold a kid's life over his father's head. That wasn't a debt you ever called in…

But for Grace, he was calling it.

Joe shook his head and drew a shaky breath. "I need a drink. Have a seat. We've got… shit to discuss." Joe gestured his hand at the Formica table in the corner, then sat down and poured himself three fingers of Irish.

Jameson's. Just like their dad had drunk.

Donnie took a seat at the table and glanced around the kitchen. The only time he'd been here, a year ago, Joe's wife Karen had had a pot roast in the oven, and the whole place had smelled homey and inviting. Their three kids had been running around, bouncing off the walls, even Declan. But tonight, the house was… quiet. Stale.

No car in the driveway. No kids making noise.

Suspicion clenched in Donnie's gut and he got up to open the refrigerator. Joe sighed, but didn't move to stop him.

Empty, except for a pitcher of water and a bunch of condiments in the door. It looked like Karen and the kids had taken off... or Joe had sent them away.

Fuck.

"Where is she, Joe?" he demanded.

"I... I'm not saying shit," Joe replied. But his eyes darted left, to the small bedroom off the kitchen.

Christ Jesus, she was *here*.

Donnie strode across the room, his eyes on his brother, but Joe didn't move except to pour the whiskey down his throat and pour himself another.

"I didn't wanna be mixed up in this shit, Don. You *know* how Mikey is," Joe whined.

Yeah, Donnie knew. That's why he'd walked away years ago rather than spend his life as Mikey's lackey. Joe had chosen differently.

Donnie turned the knob, but the door was locked. He ran his hand above the door jamb, rolling his eyes at his brother's stupidity when he found the fucking skeleton key on the first try. To Joe's credit, he clearly hadn't been trying very hard. It was almost like he'd wanted someone to find Grace.

He pushed the door open, and entered the cool, dark room.

The room was empty except for a twin bed in the corner, where a woman lay curled on her side away from him, covered by a thin blanket. He crept toward the bed slowly, his mind rapidly cycling through the best ways of transporting her. Was she drugged? How could he wake her?

Long, *long*, strands of familiar dark hair covered her face and he reached out a hand to push them aside, but he actually found himself hesitating. God, what did she look like now?

The hesitation was nearly his downfall.

The woman on the bed, who had been breathing so deeply

just a moment ago, leapt into action, grabbing his wrist and yanking him down, then delivering a powerful knee to his gut, before lunging upright and delivering a sharp blow to the back of his head that made him see stars.

Only instinct had him reaching out, ducking her flailing fists, to grab her around the waist and pull her back on the bed.

"Let go of me, asshole!" the woman screamed as she thrashed and flailed. "Or I swear to God, I will extract your motherfucking dick through your motherfucking nose!"

What?

Without wasting another moment, Donnie lifted one knee and straddled her on the bed, sitting across her thighs to neutralize her legs. He grabbed her hands in each of his and bore down, until her arms were braced above her head, and still she would not yield.

"Let. Me. *Go!*" She reared up, trying to knock her head into his.

Christ, she was amazing. Every twist of her head against the pillow had him smelling cinnamon, and every flex of her muscles reminded him that she was *here*. She was *okay*.

A weight on his chest he hadn't realized he was carrying seemed to loosen.

"Grace," he said. "Grace, baby, it's me."

Her thrashing stopped, and only the sound of harsh breathing—hers *and* his—filled the room.

"D-donnie?" Her voice was small, tentative.

"Yeah," he said.

He cautiously released one of her hands and brushed the hair back from her face.

His breath stuttered.

The only light in the room came from the streetlight shining in the window, but as her gorgeous eyes came into view, he wondered how he could ever have doubted that he'd recognize her. He'd know those eyes anywhere. But the rest of her...

The last time he'd seen Grace, she'd been on the edge of womanhood. She'd lost the sweet, rounded look she'd had as a little girl, but she'd still been stick-skinny, all knobby knees and braces. *But now...*

He swallowed hard.

She was all curves, from the pleasantly rounded hips and thighs between his knees, to the sweet, full curve of her breasts as her chest heaved under his. And damn if, all spread out on top of her like this, his dick hadn't taken notice. Time seemed suspended as he returned his gaze to her face, to those full lips that parted and begged to be kissed, to be bitten *hard*. He could imagine himself wrapping that hair around his wrist, and holding her down as he fucked her until she screamed...

She was staring up at him the way she always had, with full-on trust, like he'd hung the moon... and suddenly he felt like the sickest prick on the planet.

Control yourself. This is Grace.

"Get her out of here," Joe said from the doorway, resignation in his voice. "I told you I'd help you, but we need to figure out a plan."

Donnie nodded without turning his head, and heard Joe shuffle away.

"If I let you go, are you gonna *extract my motherfucking dick through my motherfucking nose?*" he asked, unable to look away from her face.

She giggled, and then her eyes filled with tears. For all her tough talk, she'd been scared to death, and he knew it.

"I'll try to restrain myself," she whispered.

He smiled. Then he let go of her hands and eased back. But before he could stand, she stopped him with a hand on his cheek.

"I knew when you found out you'd come, Donnie. I knew you'd keep me safe."

He closed his eyes against the warmth that seared his chest, a sensation he hadn't felt in years. That, coupled with the arousal that hadn't completely abated, had him biting back a moan.

He'd keep her safe from Mikey, but who was gonna keep this woman safe from *him*?

Chapter 2

Grace clung to the heat of Donnie's back, her legs straddling his bike as it rumbled beneath them. This couldn't be happening. She'd wake up and realize this had all been a dream, something that had started like her worst nightmare come true and ended with her here, on *his* bike, rescued by none other than the one man she'd been in love with since she was in grade school. God, how she'd wanted to be here, just like this, her arms around his broad, muscled chest, her body pressed up against his, feeling the power of his bike beneath her.

It was a sticky, hot summer day in July, the cicadas' buzzing warning that the temperature would be rising. "The sizzle bugs say it'll be hot today," her mother would say. "Make sure you keep safe, chica." Her father and mother had to work, and her brother was with his posse of friends, supposedly going to the fireworks on the beach come nightfall, but more likely planning to sneak in beer and weed and lift some skirts.

Grace, who had just turned thirteen years old, was sitting on the balcony of the third-floor apartment where her family lived. She hated the third floor when it was grocery shopping day, as it meant lugging the bags up three flights of stairs, but on days like today, when everyone was gone and she was alone, she liked it. Sitting on a worn, rusty folding chair high enough she could see over the railing, she was drawing. Humming, she was drawing on a scrap of paper she'd saved from art class at school, and a stub of a pencil she had left from a birthday present Donnie had given her the month before. Below, in the yard, rose tall stalks of summer wildflowers. But from here, her vision was obscured. She needed to get down to see them.

As she stood, she heard the riproar of a motorcycle entering the yard, and her heart did a somersault. There was only one boy who had a motorcycle on their street, and when he parked it, he'd be just on the other side of the gate in her backyard.

Kneeling behind the rail, she looked down. Would he be alone?

He was.

Her heart soared. This is when her fantasy would play out. He'd park his bike, and hop the fence, climbing the fire escape and somehow managing to swing up and come to her. But no, that wouldn't happen. She'd have to go to him.

She walked quickly through the tiny apartment, ignoring her piles of schoolbooks and the mountain of laundry her mother had asked her to fold. When she got to the first floor exit that led to the small, paved backyard, she looked to make sure he was still there. She could see his large frame through the wrought iron fence just on the other side of the yard, smoothing a rag over the gleaming handlebars. He'd saved every penny for six years to buy his first bike, and he took meticulous care of it. She didn't even want to know what kinds of jobs he'd done to earn the money, but she'd been as happy as he'd been the day he'd driven it home.

"Hey, Donnie!" she said, waving her hand to get his attention.

He turned to her, but his eyes were guarded. He looked over her shoulder and up, to the balcony of the apartment where her family lived. Her momentary glee halted as she realized who he was looking for. He wanted to be sure her father wouldn't come out and berate her for talking to "the lowlife Nolan boys." Her father hated the whole family. He reluctantly allowed Pedro to hang with Donnie, but wouldn't allow Grace.

But her father was at work, and what he didn't know wouldn't hurt him.

"You all alone today, Gracie?" he asked.

She nodded. "Mama and Papa are at work," she said, "and Pedro is doing God-knows-what. I'm supposed to stay mostly in, but it's hot, and I wanted to get a better view of the flowers I was sketching."

She suddenly remembered the paper in her hand, her flimsy excuse for running downstairs to see him, as she hid it behind her back. He stood, all six foot two inches of muscles and testosterone, the tattoos her father despised creeping along his neck and arms. Her hands trembled holding the paper as he approached the fence. He was everything a teenaged girl could dream of, and everything a teenaged girl's father hated. His faded jeans clung to his hips, a thin black t-shirt stretched taut against his chest, as he leaned against the fence and crossed his arms. His dirty-blond hair was so long it nearly hit his stubbled chin, shading his warm but intimidating chocolate-brown eyes. He made her feel things no other boy ever had, and as he leaned over the thin fence that separated them, her stomach clenched while her heart soared. She was reminded of the time she'd gone on a field trip to Niagara Falls and walked close to the edge. Fear mingled with awe, and she was dumbstruck.

He reached one large hand over the fence, his fingers clean but stained from the dirty work he did—both maintaining his bike, and whatever he did for his cousin. She didn't know exactly what his family was into or what Donnie's role was, but she knew that where he went, a wide berth followed, and she knew it was for good reason.

"Lemme see," he said, his deep voice making her shiver despite the sweltering heat.

She shook her head, holding it behind her back. She could not do this. Her family cared little for her drawings, and the kids at school mocked her.

They weren't good. She knew that, had been told so plenty of times, but she loved them.

"I'm not done," she stalled. As his eyes narrowed and his heavy blond brows drew together, she suddenly realized how very scary he could be.

"Grace," he said, warning, his growly voice and stern look making her hands shake, but still, she shook her head. His eyes softened, and his voice lowered. "Hey, it's me. You can trust me, honey."

Honey. Oh, God. A lump rose in her throat. She wanted to run and hide. She wanted to climb over the fence and kiss him.

"It's not good, Donnie," she whispered.

He smiled then, a rarity in those days, his beautiful brown eyes welcoming and kind. "Gracie," he said. "I've seen more of your drawings than anyone, and I can promise you this. If you did it, it's fucking good."

She knew then that she loved him.

"I'll make you a deal," she said, on a whim of temporary bravado. "You let me sit on your bike, and you can see it." The moment the words left her mouth, she wanted to take them back, as his eyes darkened and his jaw clenched.

"Your father would kill me, and then lock you in your house until you're thirty, and you know it," he growled.

The reminder of her father's overprotectiveness needled her temper. "Oh yeah?" she spat. "Maybe I'll wait until you're gone and sneak over and go on it myself!" she said, sounding like a bratty child even to her own ears.

His eyes narrowed even further as his voice hardened. "I catch you on my bike without my permission, I'll bend you over my knee and spank your ass, and I don't mean maybe." Though she'd heard similar threats from her older brother a million times, somehow hearing it come from Donnie's lips felt… different. His sternness made her repentant. She'd crossed a line. Though her heart was hammering and her palms were sweaty, she felt chastened. She cast her eyes down.

"I'm sorry, Donnie," she said. As a peace offering, she drew the paper

from behind her back and handed it to him. "Here. I still have a ways to go…" *she halted, but his broad hand had already gently taken the sketch from her.*

"Jesus, Gracie," *he said, his voice low and reverent now as he took in her drawing. The wildflowers bordered the edge of a creek. He could feel the movement of the water in the strokes of lines on paper, hear the caws of the crows she'd drawn tucked into the branches of pine needles.* "Not finished?" *he asked.* "How could you make something like this even better?"

"You're just saying that to be nice," *she stammered, unable to fathom that anyone could react with such emotion to something she'd created.*

He frowned, lifting his eyes to hers, as he shook his head. "Don't be ridiculous," *he said.* "I never say shit I don't mean, and you know that."

She did, she really really did. Tears pricked the back of her eyes and her nose stung.

"You know what I like about this?" *His deep voice had dropped to a whisper, as he gestured one broad finger to the drawing.*

"What?" *she whispered back.*

"You don't see the end," *he said.* "There's no mouth of a river. It's not just a little pond. The water keeps going, past the page, and you don't know where it goes to. It could go anywhere."

"Yes," *she whispered.*

"It doesn't have to stay here. And I think that water runs deep, doesn't it?"

She could only nod.

He got it.

"I'll tell you what, Gracie," *he said, reaching a hand and tucking a stray piece of hair behind her ear in a gesture that made her legs wobble beneath her.* "You let me keep this one, and I promise you. I give you my word. I'll not only let you sit on my bike, but some day, when it won't get you locked up and me murdered, I'll take you for a ride on my bike and we'll find this brook."

"Deal," *she whispered.*

. . .

She'd relived the memory so many times over the years, that thirteen years later she could still remember every vivid detail. The way he'd shooed her back into the house before her father had caught her. His threat to spank her, which had become the central focus of her fantasies over the years. How he'd taken the paper reverently and thanked her. The way the cicadas had buzzed along with the tempo of her heart, as she'd raced up the stairs back to her bedroom.

One little moment on the Fourth of July thirteen years ago that she'd never forgotten.

He had never taken her to find the creek, and today was the first time he'd taken her for the promised ride.

I had to go to some ridiculous lengths to finally get on the back of his bike, she thought. He took a left turn down a narrow, deserted street. She leaned in closer to him, inhaling the scent of leather and musk that made her toes curl.

She sobered, held on tighter, and took in her surroundings. She'd known where she was and why, held hostage in dirty Joe's near-vacant house, before Mikey Nolan's henchman would come and take her to auction. Fucking *auction*! As if she were a piece of real estate or a vintage car. Donnie'd gone north, then south again, to lose anyone tailing them, weaving in and out of traffic expertly. They were on the Zakim bridge now, lit up with lights against the evening sky, so lovely she'd have enjoyed the sight if the circumstances had been any different. For all she knew, the sons of bitches that had sent her to Joe's were pursuing them, and this was no joyride. Still, the feel of Donnie beneath her hands and pressed up against her chest, the wind that whipped her arms and legs, and the feel of the too-big helmet he'd insisted she wear, exhilarated her. She wasn't being held in a tiny prison-like room, prepared to lose her virginity to the highest bidder. She was on the back of Donnie's bike. He'd saved her.

But where were they going?

After they got off the bridge, they flew through a tunnel, road signs flashing past them. They were south of the city now. She had no idea where they were going, but had a vague recollection that Donnie lived south of Boston, somewhere near the ocean. The city behind them was alive with lights, traffic heavy, as he signaled and slowed, getting off at an exit.

Welcome to Quincy.

He said nothing as they cruised to a halt at a traffic light, but merely glanced to his left and right, likely making sure they weren't being followed.

She wasn't *that* important, was she?

Apparently, Donnie thought so.

He cruised down a road that led to an intersection, and as she took it all in. The restaurants, convenience stores, and homes that clustered the streets of the city had her realizing he was pulling onto the road that led to the beach. She breathed in the distinctive smell of the ocean, the salty breeze permeating her senses. Though it was dark, the streetlights illuminated the walking paths, where people on bicycles and joggers took a late-night ride or stroll. She heard the crashing of waves on sand, but had little time to take it all in before he was careening down a small, narrow street that was no doubt a back road. He slowed, taking one final turn onto a street marked with a green and white road sign that read *Harbor Road*.

The tempo of her heartbeat accelerated. Was he taking her to his home? She couldn't help the thrill that rippled through her.

Donnie's home.

When he pulled his bike to park, she wondered why he'd pulled up to a large brick building. It looked more like an office than an apartment complex. But she had little time to dwell as he parked. "Hold my shoulders and swing down while I hold the bike steady," he commanded. She obeyed, her hands on his broad, leather-clad shoulders as she got off the bike and stood. He dismounted, taking her helmet in his hand and gesturing for her to go up the back stairs. She tried to take a look around, and thought she saw what looked like the bar and dance floor of a club, but he didn't allow her to stop and sightsee as he hurried her along.

"Third floor," he ground out. "*Go.*"

As she walked up the stairs, she saw drops of blood in front of her, crimson stains on the light woodwork. Bile rose in her throat. *God.* What had happened? But she couldn't think on the details, as he was following behind her like the hounds of hell were on her heels. One step after another, and finally he pulled a large key ring from his pocket, shoved a key in the door in front of her, and pushed her through. "Get *in,*" he growled.

Both hurt and anger stung her as she obeyed. Where was her knight in shining armor, and who was this rough, angry man who now loomed over her in the dim light of the tiny kitchen? He shut the door behind them, locked it, and threw the deadbolt, before shrugging out of his leather jacket. He reached his hands to her, and before she knew what he was doing, he deftly removed her jacket as well.

Slinging both jackets on the back of a chair, he took her by the hand and pulled her through the small, spartan kitchen. Before they exited she got a glimpse of a gleaming Keurig in the corner, and a row of little coffee pods ready to go, and a small bowl of fruit, but nothing else.

Directly adjacent to the kitchen, to the right, was a tiny bathroom. She caught a glimpse of a mirror and sink before he yanked her hand harder, and she had to practically jog to keep up with him. A small sitting room housed a loveseat and flat-screened TV mounted on the wall in one corner, and in the other corner was a weight bench and a stack of free weights. To the left was a doorway she assumed led to a bedroom. He smacked it open with the flat of his palm.

God almighty.

Donnie's bedroom.

In her wildest fantasies as a teen and then young adult, she'd imagined being brought into the sanctuary of Donnie's bedroom, but the circumstances had always been wildly different.

He released her hand and pulled her to his bed, pushing her so she was seated and he stood towering over her. His eyes flashed, the brows drawn together, and she noted not surprisingly that the years they'd been apart had aged him well… very, *very* well. His hair was still long, dirty-blond, and sun-streaked, but his beard was fuller. His eyes were still… *Donnie*—kind, intelligent, but ruthless, with the scar above his left eyebrow he'd have until the day he died. She knew how he got that scar, and the memory pained her. He was broader now, his wide shoulders stretching the thin cotton of his t-shirt, tats now trailing along his neck, across both shoulders, tucked under his t-shirt, then gracing both biceps and forearms. He stood with his feet apart, hands on hips and he looked fucking pissed.

What had she done? What had she *ever* done to deserve him looking so furious? "Where did they touch you? Are you hurt? How long have you been gone?" he said through clenched teeth, breathing deeply in, his chest heaving as his eyes raked over her, from the top of her head, down over her face, and she was pleased to note they momentarily halted over the expanse of her chest before taking in the rest of her body with an appraising but fairly appreciative glance.

"It's hard to remember everything. My head hurts," she said, putting one hand out with her palm facing him, trying to calm his fury. "They came after dark yesterday and took me from my home. Mama was at work, so I was alone, sleeping. I have a shift at work tomorrow." She knew she was babbling, but couldn't seem to stop. "All I knew was there were three masked men who bound and dragged me out, and they must've drugged me or knocked me unconscious, because the next thing I knew I was in that bed at your brother's house. There were men there, and they were scary, so I didn't fight. I couldn't win, just me against a bunch of guys with weapons."

One curt nod, and he stepped toward her, leaning one knee on the bed as his big, gentle hands probed her head. His voice had softened when he spoke. "You *had* a shift tomorrow." She didn't respond, not knowing what to say, as he continued. "Where exactly does it hurt, Gracie?"

She closed her eyes momentarily and swallowed. *Gracie.* No one had called her that in years. As she pointed to the back of her head, his tenderness caused a lump to rise in her throat.

"You'll need ice," he murmured. "And I'll get you some pain meds. They didn't touch you anywhere else?" Though he wore a mask of self-control, the forced tightness in his voice betrayed him. He hadn't been mad at her. He'd been mad *for* her. God, he still cared. After all these years, *he still cared.*

Then why had he left her?

"Nowhere else," she whispered.

His hands rested on her shoulders. "Nowhere else," he

repeated. "Sons of bitches. I'd kill them, Gracie, every last motherfucker. They'll never lay hands on you again."

She suspected she knew what it cost for him to say it. He'd moved on, no longer a part of the family who bullied and took over all of South Boston. He'd moved past this life, and now he was being dragged back in. For her.

"They didn't, Donnie," she whispered, laying a hand on one of his. "I'm fine."

"Yeah," he said. "And I'm gonna make sure you stay that way." He sighed and pushed himself to standing. He paced the room, running his hands through his hair, and she took the moment to observe her surroundings. She was on a king-sized bed, but the size of the bed was the only thing in the room even slightly decadent. In the left corner of the room stood a bureau, as tall as she was, with four drawers, plain, utilitarian light wood. No mirror, nothing on top. A door to a closet was to the right of the bed, but it was shut tight. To the right of the bed, a nightstand flanked the bed, with nothing but a lamp and a small basket filled with coins. There was nothing else in the entire room. No pictures were on the walls, no books on a shelf or shoes pushed up against the wall.

He was like a golden-haired, tattooed, muscled monk living a spartan existence.

Was this his *home*?

"I'm gonna lay it all on the line with you, Grace," he said. "Pedro came by earlier."

Pedro. Her mind immediately went back to the drops of blood on his stairway. She'd suspected somehow Pedro was behind this.

Donnie continued. "He told me they had you. Do you have any idea why?"

She shook her head. "I know he's in debt with Mikey," she

said. Mikey, Donnie's cousin, the low-life asshole who preyed on young women, and made his living off pawned possessions and broken dreams. He'd grown so rich while trampling on those under him, he thought he ruled the world. She didn't want to discuss more with him, not after he'd tried so hard to shake off everything he grew up with.

He crossed his arms on his chest and raised a brow to her. "That the truth, Grace?" The stern look made her insides quiver as she shifted on the bed, immediately reminding her of the scene she'd played over in her mind hundreds of times, his threat to take her over his knee. He was strong, dominant, the most alpha of the bunch she'd grown up with, and she'd wondered what he'd do if she pushed him.

She swallowed. "That's the truth."

His eyes narrowed. "You do not want to lie to me, Grace."

She shifted on the bed, again, feeling the implied threat right between her legs. *Fuck*, she was still hot for him.

She swallowed. "Nothing else," she said.

Donnie nodded again. "I'll take care of this," he said. Her heart twisted, and she briefly closed her eyes. He was in, and he didn't want to be.

"Okay," she whispered. "You wanna fill me in on where we are?"

In response, he sat next to her and lifted one boot-clad foot to his knee, untying the laces as he looked down, not meeting her gaze. "I work here," he said. "We have security cameras, bouncers, and you'll be under my protection. It's the safest place for you."

Warmth spread in her chest, and she was almost glad she'd been in danger.

Under my protection. It's the safest place for you.

But hold the phone. He worked here? At a club? She'd assumed he only rented the apartment.

"What do you do here?" she asked.

He cleared his throat, switched feet, and started unlacing the second boot. He didn't answer at first. His reluctance to tell her everything made her uneasy. Was he afraid? What was he hiding? He didn't trust her? God, did he have a girlfriend? Or a *wife?*

"So, great," she said, feeling her heartbeat quicken and her temperature rise. "You want me to spill all, and you don't even have the balls to tell me where we are?"

The second the words left her mouth, she regretted them. He gently placed his boot on the floor, and turned his body fully to face her, one brow raised in reproach as his lips turned down in a scowl. *God*, he could be scary. She squirmed on the bed, involuntarily pulling away a bit.

"Yeah," he said. "That's exactly right, little girl. I'm not telling you where we are because I'm afraid. Shaking in my fucking boots." His gritty tone left no doubt his response dripped with sarcasm. Donnie Nolan was many things, but fearful was not one of them.

"I need to know," she said, but her plea was weaker this time, losing the edge of reproach.

He sighed. "I know you do, and I'll tell you. But I'm still not sure how much you need to know, and what's safest for you. The less you know about some things, the better."

What was *that* supposed to mean?

"Whatever," she mumbled, earning her a second reproachful look.

Something in her response made his eyes narrow again, and he skewered her with a stern look, before he sighed. "Fine, Grace. It might help you a bit to know where we are, so I'll tell you. This is The Club South, which I operate and manage. It's a satellite location of The Club. Do you know what The Club is?"

She shook her head.

He sighed. "The Club is the largest BDSM club in the northeast."

Her eyes widened. "BDSM?" Oh *my*.

He pursed his lips and nodded. "Yep. BDSM. Blake Coleman, Matteo Angelico, and Alex Slater are the owners, and I'm the operator. I oversee this location, after working for years at The Club in Boston. Blake taught me everything he knows, and after I tasted the scene, I wanted in. So I've got this club up and running, and I'm part of the operation team, too."

"Operation team?" What exactly did *that* mean?

He smirked. "Yeah. Operation team. That means I work as dungeon master here. I do demonstrations."

Her voice sounded unnaturally high-pitched. "Demonstrations?"

He paused a beat before answering, his brow quirked menacingly. "Yeah, Gracie. Demonstrations." A slow, wicked grin, lit up his face. "That means I like to tie girls up and spank their asses. That means I call the shots, and I fucking love it. I like the control, and I fully plan on keeping it that way."

Hoooooly *shit*.

"Well then," she said, because she didn't have a clue how else to respond.

He grinned again. "Not your thing, huh?"

Not her thing? She didn't even know what it was or how one did things or what exactly was *demonstrated* in a *demonstration*, but if it involved Donnie? Then yeah.

It was her thing.

She shrugged. "No idea," she said. "But I think it's sorta cool that it's *your* thing." The whole idea was sort of intriguing. "You gonna let me see you demonstrate?"

He shook his head. "No *way.*"

"Aw, c'mon, Donnie," she said. "I want to... see that side of you."

It all made sense. Of course he was into control. He thrived as the one in charge. He was a naturally dominant guy, and did not willingly submit to anyone's authority. Hell, it was why he left school at the ripe old age of fifteen, and why he'd been promoted as the enforcer for his cousin the following month. No one fucked with Donnie Nolan.

"Not now, Grace," was all he said.

"Makes sense, you know," she said. "You never followed everyone else's rules. You aren't the kind of guy who does. And I could..." She faltered as the image of Donnie tying her up flew through her mind. She swallowed. "I could totally see you being the one in charge like that."

To her surprise, he chuckled. "Yeah, well. Anyway, we weren't followed." He paused. "According to Joe, Mikey planned to stash you with him for a week. That gives us a few days to regroup and figure out how we're going to play this."

He stood, taking his boots to his closet and putting them outside the door. "Until then?" He turned around and pointed a finger at her. "You *do not move.*"

Wait—*what?*

"I don't move?" she said, frowning. "Like, from this bed? Are you out of your *mind?* I have to, you know, at least use the bathroom or get something to eat."

His brown eyes grew cloudy, brooding, as he stalked back over to her. When he reached her, he grasped her shoulders in his huge, hot, powerful hands, and shook her, not harshly, but enough that she stopped talking and looked up at him with wide, curious eyes. She swallowed.

"I mean this apartment. You'll stay inside. Do not push me, Grace," he said, and she wondered suddenly if this was his... *master* voice, or whatever it was called. His serious one.

"Donnie," she said pleadingly, trying to get his attention. "You can't keep me locked in a tower like this. I can't just... stay in this little apartment."

He glowered at her. "For now, you can," he said. "Until I figure out what's going on, and can get a man on you at all times, you stay here. No going home. You do not leave this apartment without my permission."

Permission?

She pulled back and crossed her arms on her chest. "Since when did I say you had the right to demand I ask permission for anything?"

His eyes narrowed further and to her shock, he leaned in, pulling her hair back, not too harshly, but enough that her breath caught in her throat.

"Since I pulled you out of Joe's fucking house to save you from being on *auction*, Grace. And you want to see a demonstration? You want to see what I'm like as a dom? You disobey me, and you'll get every bit of demonstration your ass can handle."

Chapter 3

She was in his shower.

Donnie was valiantly trying to focus on all the paperwork he needed to get done for his business meeting with Blake and the guys tomorrow, while waiting for phone calls from Joe and Pedro, and steeling himself to deal with the deep, *deep* pile of shit he'd swan-dived into last night, but all he could think of was Grace. How he'd gone back to his apartment to grab clothes after his early-morning workout, bringing her a pack of her favorite cinnamon gum and a bagel he'd grabbed for her at Dunkies, and had heard the water running in his bathroom.

How she was right now, standing behind his shower curtain, rivulets of water running over her satin skin, slicking *his* body wash over her curves and between her thighs. She'd carry his scent for the rest of the day. Would she think about him? Imagine him coming to join her? How easily he could throw back the curtain, and...

"Donnie! Yo, earth to Don!"

Villi, the head contractor on the reconstruction project was standing in front of Donnie's desk, waving a giant hand in front of Donnie's face to get his attention, while Villi's skinny, redheaded assistant, who looked and acted about twelve, raised a clipboard over his face to hide his snicker.

Buncha assholes.

Donnie raised one eyebrow and glared pointedly at Villi's hand, wordlessly inviting him to wave it just one more fucking time... so Donnie could rip it off and stick it somewhere more appropriate.

Villi's face broke into a broad grin, totally unperturbed by Donnie's glare, possibly since he was built like a fucking Viking—tall, blond, and ready to bench-press a pickup truck.

Donnie sighed. "You think it's a good idea to come into my office without knocking?" he demanded.

"Door was open and I *did* knock. Called your name a bunch too," Villi said cheerfully, his blue eyes twinkling. "Not to mention, I texted you an hour ago and told you I'd be by to review the bids for the exterior work and the security system upgrade. You said, and I quote, *Okay.*" He smirked at Donnie, then elbowed his assistant. "Looks like *somebody* had a hell of a night last night, eh, Gib?"

"Oh, yeah. A hell of a night, all right," Donnie agreed drily, shaking his head. And it had been, just not at all in the fun way they were thinking... unless somehow huddling on the too-small couch in his living room, unable to sleep because he was hard as a boulder, but steadfastly refusing to jerk off to images of the pissed-off virgin he'd locked in his bedroom, was their idea of a good time. It definitely wasn't Donnie's.

"I think Donnie musta *tied some girl up* and gotten *the business!*" the kid snickered, as though this were the most deviant and outlandish thing he could accuse Donnie of. If he only knew.

Donnie rolled his eyes. Gib hadn't stopped snickering since

the moment he'd heard The Club was actually a *BDSM club* where *(gasp!)* people had sex. Donnie couldn't remember ever being that young or that innocent.

"Leave the bids," Donnie told Villi, nodding towards the mostly-tidy surface of his desk. "I'll review 'em with Blake tomorrow. We're gonna need to add some serious exterior lighting for the back entrance."

Villi nodded, pushing his thick, blond hair off his forehead. "Already noted."

Donnie grunted, not surprised that Villi had anticipated this need. He trusted Villi and his team to be professional and discreet, even skinny, freckle-faced Gib.

"And what about the fucking fire alarm?" Donnie demanded. "Damn thing went off twice this week for no apparent reason. Blaring alarm and a buncha fire trucks rolling down the street at three in the morning isn't the best way to get to know the new neighbors."

Villi frowned. "Oh, yeah, I got your message on that. I'll take a peek this week, but it's not uncommon for a new system to be a little glitchy. Settings need to be adjusted and that sort of thing, especially if there's a heat source near any of the sensors."

Donnie nodded, and the men took off, leaving a folder of bids on the desk as they walked away. Donnie grabbed it, absently rifling through the papers inside without seeing them.

Donnie musta tied some girl up.

He snorted to himself. Sorry to disappoint you, Gib, but in this case, the girl's got *me* tied up. And wasn't *that* a kick in the balls?

His Gracie, the sweet little girl with the big eyes that had seen clear down to his soul, the ghost who had haunted his memories for the last decade, was all grown up. And in her place was a gorgeous spitfire of a woman with a sinfully lush body who seemed hell-bent on pushing every fucking one of his buttons.

God. He threw the folder down on his desk, grabbed his empty coffee cup, and stalked to the mini kitchen near the desk where his receptionist would sit… once he hired one. He was not caffeinated enough to deal with thoughts of Grace yet. He grabbed the high-octane blend he preferred from the little whirly thing next to the coffee maker and set it to brew.

Donnie didn't smoke, hadn't had a joint since high school, and hadn't been drunk in years—not since he'd found The Club and Blake had taken him under his wing. Donnie had learned from Blake's example that *real* men didn't go around bragging about the booze they drank, the ass they tapped, and the money in their accounts. It was a lesson his hotheaded younger self had learned slowly and painfully, but permanently.

So he worked out religiously and ate clean when he wasn't road-tripping. He avoided fights and messy entanglements. He didn't gamble. He kept his checkbook balanced. He'd restored his bike himself, and kept it meticulously tuned up. He had friends, but he relied on himself. Caffeine, and lots of it, was his one true vice. (Well, if you didn't count the whips, the clamps, the ropes, and the way he got off on inflicting just the right amount of pain and humiliation in a scene. But around here, that pretty much passed for normal, which was one of the things he loved about it.)

So it was all the more stunning when he looked back at his behavior the previous night. When was the last time he'd been goaded into losing control like he had last night?

I like to tie girls up and spank their asses.

Jesus. It was the truth, and he wasn't ashamed of it. But that area of his life, the kink he enjoyed, had not one fucking *thing* to do with Grace Diaz, no matter how well she'd filled out, no matter how her beautiful eyes still seemed to see things inside him that no one else saw, and no matter how much she fired his blood. If Pedro was right, she was still a fucking *virgin*, for Christ's sake.

He'd told himself in the moment that he was warning her off, scaring her away. *Shut the fuck up with your stupid taunts and your innocent questions. I'm not the man you think I am. I never was.*

But Grace was the one person he'd always communicated with almost instinctively, and as he'd lain awake on his living room sofa in the darkness, he'd admitted to himself that the words hadn't been a warning, but a challenge.

You wanted her to offer herself to you.

Wrong as it was, selfish as it was, maybe he had.

He'd been off his game from the moment he'd found her on that shitty little bed in Joe's spare room, or… hell, even before that. He hadn't been himself since the moment her brother had spoken her name last night. All Donnie's control had evaporated, and the easygoing facade he usually employed effortlessly had disappeared. Instead he'd been a creature driven by instinct. *Find her. Protect her. Keep her safe.*

Because the truth was, there were other places he could take Grace besides The Club. One call to Lucas, and Grace could be sharing a room at a safehouse with her brother. One call to Slay, and Grace could be whisked out of the state, out of Mikey's reach. And if he were truly a man who was in control and thinking logically, he'd make those calls.

The way his gut pulsed at the very idea confirmed that logic played no part in his thinking right now. He couldn't bear to have her where he couldn't protect her. Not now. Not again.

His phone started to chime from somewhere on his desk, and

he grabbed his coffee as he made his way back and accepted the call, with the sinking feeling that his day was about to get exponentially worse.

He knocked on the door to his apartment and waited for a moment before putting his key in the lock and pushing it open, bracing himself for a confrontation with the angry woman he'd left behind the night before.

Instead, after a quick glance at the kitchen and sitting area, he found Grace sitting cross-legged in the center of his bed, his headphones in her ears, as she strummed her thighs in time to the music on the shitty, old iPod he sometimes used while working out. She was wearing her jeans from last night, and a shirt she must have taken from his dresser. It was five sizes too big, and though she'd knotted it at her waist, it still hung off one bare shoulder, exposing the smooth golden skin of her arm and the upper slope of her breast.

He swallowed.

She was reading a magazine, an old issue of *Cycle World* he had kicking around, like it was fascinating literature. Her long hair was up in a turban made from one of his towels, and her face was scrubbed clean, both of makeup and of the pissy, defensive expression she'd been wearing the night before. *This* was his Grace. This, right here, was the girl he knew. And he leaned against the doorframe for a minute to watch her.

A moment later, her brow furrowed at whatever she was reading and she tapped her lip thoughtfully. He stifled a laugh.

"What's so interesting?" he asked, moving further into the

room and closing the door behind him. The woman was like a magnet, and everything about her called to him.

She startled and blushed like he'd caught her reading *Playboy* instead of *Cycle World*, and grabbed the earbuds out of her ears.

"Donnie! I… we have to talk about…"

He stalked towards her, watching her put her defensive mask back in place, and not liking it one bit.

"What article were you reading?" he demanded again, pausing beside the bed and peering down. She was flustered, her cheeks blushing a deep rose as he leaned closer.

"It's, uh, about an Indian Roadmaster Classic," she read from the title. "It looks kinda retro and… *uh!*"

The last word came out more like a squeak as he put a knee down on the bed behind her, levering himself close enough to read over her shoulder.

He was entirely *too* close right now, and alarm bells went off in his head, warning him that he was playing a risky fucking game, but he ignored them. From the moment he'd seen her sitting on his bed, he'd wanted to get closer, to see if she smelled like *his* Gracie—all cinnamon bubblegum innocence—or like the sexy woman he'd imagined this morning, using his shower and smelling like his soap.

"Retro *and…*" he prompted, his nose just a millimeter above her bare shoulder. She shuddered delicately, maybe at his breath on her skin, or maybe just his nearness, but either way, as he watched her nipple pebble beneath the thin cotton of his t-shirt, for the second time in as many days, he felt his control snap.

"Hot," she finished in a whisper, at the exact moment that his open mouth landed on her skin.

If forbidden fruit always tasted this sweet, Donnie understood what had happened with Adam and Eve. Because as he moved his tongue along the column of her throat, tasting the frantic beat of her pulse, her high-pitched moan of encouragement, and the trusting way she tilted her head to the side, yielding herself to him utterly, he couldn't conjure any concept of right and wrong, good and evil. There was simply Grace, and the pure, perfect connection that had always existed between them.

He trailed open-mouthed kisses up over her jaw, the day-old growth of his beard rough against her cheek. She lifted her hand to grab a handful of his hair, holding him more tightly against her and he growled. Without conscious thought, he moved his arm around her waist, and reached his hand up to palm her breast, gently abrading the stiff peak. She caught her lip between her teeth and threw back her head, knocking the towel loose. Fragrant, damp hair spilled down her back, and her breathing hitched.

"Christ," he breathed, inhaling sharply. "*Jesus Christ.*"

Lost to the moment, lost to *her*, he moved his mouth to her ear, sucking on her lobe. His fingers pinched her nipple tightly and her back bowed, thrusting her breast more firmly into his hand. He needed to claim her, mark her, *own* her. He grasped her earlobe between his teeth and bit down firmly.

"Ow!"

That one word, that single, shocked sound of pain, had him jumping off the bed and scowling in an instant.

What the fuck was he doing?

He stared at the door, willing his heartbeat to slow and his erection to disappear. *Fucking unlikely.* He clenched his hands into fists and stalked from the room.

Get it together, asshole.

"Donnie!" Grace said, trailing after him into the living area, her voice pleading, confused, and aroused. "I-I'm sorry, I...You just startled me."

"You got nothin' to be sorry for, Gracie." His voice was rough and unsteady. "That was..." He scrubbed his hand through his hair, trying to find a word, but for maybe the first time with Grace, his mind stuttered and blanked, and he said the first thing that came to his mind. "A mistake. A stupid mistake."

She inhaled sharply and he turned around to see her jaw harden and her eyes flare.

"No, it wasn't."

He blinked. She spoke with an absolute confidence that shocked him. She was a virgin, for God's sake, and he'd manhandled her. *Him*. A guy she hadn't seen in years, a man who was nearly a perfect stranger to her. He'd felt her up, used his tongue and his teeth on her flesh. He'd expected more outrage, or at the very least, hesitation. She showed neither.

Had someone kissed her like that before?

It shouldn't have mattered, but he couldn't stop himself from thinking about it. Was she really the virgin that Mikey believed her to be?

His cock was extremely invested in this line of thought, and he forced himself to turn away from her again, to pace to the tiny kitchen area and contemplate brewing another cup of coffee. *Virgin or not, she's not interested in the kind of shit you like.*

He changed the subject. "So, I talked to Pedro this morning," he said over his shoulder, as though nothing had happened.

"Yeah? Lucky *you*." Her voice was sullen in a way he'd never heard from her before, and he wondered whether it was from their kiss—their *mistake*—or the mention of her brother. Either way it pissed him off. Made him want to spank that bitchy attitude right out of her.

He clutched the handle of his coffee mug until his knuckles turned white, but couldn't resist scolding. "Hey. He's worried about you. Told him you were safe."

She snorted. "*Safe*. 'Cause that's all that really matters, right?"

Surprise made him turn to look at her. "What's that supposed to mean?"

She threw herself down on the sofa in the living area, and stared at the ceiling. "Nothing. Never mind."

Christ. He wanted to hold her down and tan her ass so badly that his palm was literally tingling. "Enough of this shitty attitude, angel. I asked you a fucking question."

She glared across the room at him. "Oh, now you want an answer? Now I'm your angel? Is now finally a convenient time for you to hear what *I* have to say? I've been locked in this apartment for eighteen hours. Prisoners of war get better treatment."

His head went back in shock. Who *was* this bad-tempered, defensive woman?

"Jesus! You're pissed that I've been a bad host? Was the fuckin' bed not comfortable enough, your highness? Not enough reading material at your disposal? Apologies that I was busy keeping you *alive*."

She laughed bitterly and he fought another flare of surprise. The Grace he'd known didn't know how to be bitter. "Alive and safe," she repeated. "Is that all that's supposed to matter? Safe and alive and *alone* isn't much of a life. And newsflash, Donnie. I haven't been safe since the day you walked out of the neighborhood."

A cold feeling gripped his stomach. "Explain."

She set her jaw and glared at him for a long moment, before letting out a deep sigh and relenting.

"Pedro's not the same guy he used to be," she admitted.

"Back when you were still at home, Mikey had you guys running errands and taking bets for Joe, helping him make book. But after the stuff that happened..." She glanced at him, at the scar above his eyebrow, significantly, and Donnie nodded. *After Mikey tried to promote them from head-crackers to assassins.* He wasn't likely to forget. "Nothing was the same."

Donnie took his coffee and headed into the tiny living area. He would *not* sit next to her on the couch. Instead, he straddled the weight bench on the other side of the room and gave her a tiny nod, asking her to continue.

"P was so full of himself. Mikey made a big deal out of celebrating his loyalty, you know? And P just ate it up. I think... I think he'd been jealous of you," she told him, meeting his eyes cautiously. "You were Mikey's cousin, his *blood*, and Pedro knew he was only there because you'd made it a package deal. He was always just gonna be *that Hispanic kid who hangs with Donnie Nolan.* But suddenly now *he* was Mikey's guy. He woulda done anything Mikey asked after that... *and he did.*"

Donnie felt a cold chill pass through him.

"Mikey's paranoid. From what I've heard, he always was," she said with a shrug. "But over the last few years, it got worse. Suddenly, there was no one he could trust. Nobody was loyal enough. Not Pedro, not even Joe. He needed leverage on everyone, the kind that would ensure no one would ever betray him. And *I* was part of his leverage on Pedro."

Her voice was stark and hollow. He wanted to go to her, to comfort her, but he knew he would never be able to stop with a single hug. She took a shuddering breath and continued.

"Mikey decided that I was untouchable. Not allowed to date, not allowed to leave the neighborhood, even for work. Told the guys I was some kind of honorary Nolan, and he'd marry me off to one of the family eventually, like this was medieval times and I was gonna make some marriage alliance. You believe that shit?" She laughed, but it wasn't funny.

Donnie shook his head. He really *couldn't* believe it. Mikey had always been a psychotic asshole, but *this?* His mind swirled with regret. He'd thought it would be for the best for everyone if he stayed away, that he'd been keeping everyone safe. Now it seemed like he'd left them at the mercy of a madman.

He stood up to pace the small room and turned on her. "Why didn't you leave? Mikey might think he's all-powerful in the neighborhood, in the city of Boston, but you know he's got no pull if you got far enough away. God, baby, why didn't you just fucking *leave?*"

"Yeah, leaving's pretty easy, huh?" she demanded, scraping her long hair back from her temples with both hands. "Just pack up your shit and disappear for a year... or *a dozen?*"

God, she killed him. Did she really believe he'd walked away without scars? That exile from his family and friends, from *her*, hadn't cut him deeply? He shook his head. "You think leaving was *easy?* Leaving everyone I ever knew, the only home I'd ever had, with nothing but the shirt on my back? Not even a fucking high school diploma to my name?"

She swallowed and looked away. "Maybe not *easy*. But you managed to do it, didn't you?" she whispered. She squared her shoulders, and when she spoke again, her voice was angry once more. "I couldn't. My mom lives and works in the neighborhood, remember? We have no money in the bank, no contacts anywhere, no way to get a decent job. My family in Puerto Rico is all gone now, too. And even if, by some miracle, I'd found a way to leave? Well. If I was Mikey's leverage on Pedro, I guess you could say Pedro was Mikey's leverage on me."

She took a deep breath and leaned forward, bracing her elbows on her knees. "Mikey has evidence of Pedro committing a bunch of crimes. Shit he did for *Mikey*, under Mikey's authority, but, of course, there's no paper trail. If I didn't toe the line and behave myself, and if I breathed a word to Pedro about it, Mikey would have an anonymous source deliver the evidence to the police. He told me, 'Be a good girl, Grace, and your brother will be fine.' *Be a good girl.* Just like my dad used to say when he'd keep me locked in the apartment, watching summer pass by from that shitty third-floor balcony. Just like Pedro used to tell me when I was back in high school and I'd talk about moving away and finding you again." Her voice cracked when she continued, "I'm so tired of being a good girl, Donnie, I can't even fucking tell you."

Donnie shook his head wordlessly, while those words played over in his mind. *I'm so tired of being a good girl, Donnie.*

"But I played the part anyway," she said brokenly "I got up, I went to my job, I took care of my mom. I toed the line. And what the fuck do I have to show for it?" She spread her arms wide, a gesture that encompassed Donnie's tiny apartment, her borrowed clothing, and the nuclear bomb that Pedro had dropped on her life. "My idiot brother manages to fuck up anyway, gets himself in debt to Mikey, without a single thought for the consequences to Mama or to me. Mikey decides I'm no longer untouchable, I'm fucking *property*, and he's gonna auction me off. And now I'm alone. I can't go home. I have no skills and no friends to help me." Her smile was wry as she concluded, "You'll have to pardon me if I have a shitty attitude."

He took a single step toward the sofa, and crouched down in front of her. God, but her face was beautiful. He pushed a strand of her hair back from her face with his index finger, knowing that if he touched her skin, he'd never be able to stop.

"*I* will help you," he said, his voice deep and serious. And though the idea of sending her away when he'd finally gotten to see her again caused a physical pain in his chest, he forced himself to continue. "I've got friends I can call who can relocate you and Pedro, your mom too. I've got some cash stashed away, and it's yours. Listen to me, Grace. I promised you when you were ten years old that I would always protect you, and I will."

Then he let his voice go deeper, sterner. "But I asked you last night if you knew more about this situation than *just* P being in debt to Mikey. You didn't tell me the truth."

She shuddered at the threat he let hang in the air.

"You left that life behind years ago, and I didn't want to drag you back in anymore than you already were," she said simply. The look she gave him, the way those gorgeous brown eyes held his, flayed him to the core. "You know, I understood why you had to go. You did the right thing, and I was even proud of you for going. You always were my hero. I just... wished you'd taken me with you." Her mouth twisted into a half-smile.

"Ridden away with your thirteen-year-old self on the back of my motorcycle?" He shook his head at the image.

Her smile was more genuine now. "Yes! Total hero montage, while the sappy music played." But then she shook her head. "I'm not leaving town, Donnie. I'm not running away. I can't take the chance that Mikey will hand the evidence against Pedro to the authorities and land P in prison, and he *would*, you know he would, just to be an asshole. And... I don't want to live my life in fear, always looking over my shoulder and wondering if today will be the day that Mikey catches up to me. I want to find a way to fix this. *Please.*"

He stood up and took a step back, but he couldn't look away. Inside, his desire to protect her was waging war against something even deeper—a desire to give her the life she always should've had. A life where she wasn't always locked in a tower, but was free to be truly herself and to make her own choices.

You always were my hero.

He prayed that this time he wouldn't let her down.

"Master Nolan?"

Donnie glanced up from inspecting the equipment he'd selected for his demonstration tonight, expecting to see Carly, the submissive who'd volunteered to participate in the scene. But instead of the tall, cheerful blonde, he found *Julie* standing in the doorway of the demonstration room.

Just what he absolutely *did not* need to deal with.

His voice was colder than usual as he said, "Can I help you, Julie?"

The woman shifted her feet and licked her lips suggestively, tossing her long, brown hair behind her.

Donnie raised an eyebrow. If she was attempting to pique Donnie's arousal, she was failing mightily. Julie couldn't hold a candle to the girl he'd ordered under no uncertain terms not to set foot out of his apartment upstairs.

"Julie, I'm really busy," he growled impatiently. "You're scheduled on the bar right now, and my demonstration is going to begin in ten minutes."

And not a second too soon. He was clearheaded enough to maintain total control of the scene, but he'd be lying if he didn't admit that he was looking forward to the opportunity to blow off steam… somewhat more than usual.

Primal instinct, vicious and clawing as a rabid animal, had been straining against the leash of his control all day, demanding that he either go back upstairs and finish the seduction he'd started… or else march Grace out of Boston to safety right *this minute*, gagged and trussed up in Shibari ropes if she refused to comply.

"That's what I needed to talk to you about," Julie said. "Um, Carly went home sick."

Donnie raised an eyebrow. "Sick?"

She shrugged innocently and wrinkled her nose. "Stomach thing. Vomiting. Came on her really suddenly. So weird."

Fuck. He'd have to go see about finding a replacement, and it wouldn't be easy. Most of the women who worked at The Club South weren't into open, public demonstrations when they chose to play, but preferred to keep things private. Still, maybe he could find someone.

His thoughts turned to Grace, who was right now sitting in his apartment, watching TV on his sofa. *I'm tired of being a good girl…*

He swallowed against the image that leapt to his mind of Grace, splayed out on the padded leather spanking bench he'd placed in the center of the room, ready and eager for him to cane her, to mark her.

He inhaled sharply. *Never going to happen.*

"Thanks for letting me know," he told Julie, turning back to his inspection and dismissing her.

In his peripheral vision, he saw her hesitate, twirling a lock of hair around her finger and watching him avidly. "I, um, checked around already. None of the other girls working tonight are into demos, and especially not for caning," Julie continued, confirming his fears. "But... *I am*."

Her voice was soft and husky, and Donnie ground his teeth together. *Goddamn it.* "Julie, we already discussed..."

"I understand," she told him, taking a step forward and clasping her hands in front of her chest. "You said you're not really into me, so this scene won't be personal for you. That's fine. I just want to help out, Master Nolan. I really love this job, remember?"

He turned and stared at her with narrowed eyes, searching for any sign that she wanted more from him than the endorphin rush that most submissives achieved with a good caning, but her expression was neutral and she kept her eyes on the floor.

"You know caning scenes are intense," he warned her, but she nodded.

"I know," she assured him. "I'm into it."

He gave one quick nod. Listening to a submissive, establishing limits, and trusting her to give her consent without second-guessing was an ingrained aspect of his role as a dominant.

"Talk to Connie," he said, referring to the domme who would be handling the floor while he was doing the demonstration. "Sign the forms. Be back here in five."

She nodded and scurried away excitedly.

By the time she returned a few minutes later and positioned herself on the spanking bench, a group of onlookers had already flowed into the room, quietly talking and chatting as they waited for the demo to start.

The demonstrations at The Club were always popular, even when they were held on a random Tuesday evening. Tonight, Donnie would peg about half of the observers as voyeurs who enjoyed the spectacle, and the other half as dominants looking to build on their skills. He nodded to himself, pleased. To his mind, a good dominant always wanted to learn more, always sought to improve his technique.

"Welcome to The Club," he began, his voice deliberately low and intimate. "I'm Master Nolan, and this is going to be a caning demonstration. First, I'll explain everything I'll be doing, then I'll get into the demo itself. Out of respect for me and our volunteer, Julie, you'll need to keep quiet. No interruptions during the demonstration, yeah? If you need to leave at any point, go ahead. If you have questions about implements, technique, positioning, or anything else, I'm happy to answer after we're done."

Everyone in the crowd easily nodded their assent. This was an established practice in the BDSM world, and one of the first rules that club-goers learned was the taboo of interfering with a scene.

Donnie took the crowd through the routine he planned to use.

"Before beginning, it's important to determine the *purpose* of the caning, which will determine the number and severity of the strokes you're gonna be using. Caning has a reputation for being a pretty effective form of punishment…"

He saw one man, a dominant, raise an eyebrow and exchange a pointed glance with the woman beside him. The woman lowered her eyes and flushed in a way that made Donnie suppress a smile. Clearly the woman was well aware of the cane's effectiveness.

"But if you use gentler taps, the kind that don't bend the cane," he continued, "and you space 'em well apart, both in timing and placement, caning can actually be a very sensual experience. It focuses a submissive's attention like no other punishment I've found."

He saw one or two people's eyes narrow thoughtfully, and he smiled. He fucking loved his job.

"It's important for a dominant to establish his or her submissive's pain threshold in advance—this is not an activity for first-timers. And as most doms know, starting off with a hand-spanking and/or paddling will help your submissive handle the caning better and for longer," he told them. Then he briefly took them through the specifics of positioning for both dominant and submissive to ensure the strikes landed in the proper place and serious damage didn't occur.

Once his spiel was over, though, he turned away from the crowd and trained his attention exclusively on Julie. Whatever strain might exist in their relationship outside of this room, in here, for this moment, he was her dominant and he had a responsibility to focus on her needs, her responses, her tolerance, and getting her where she needed to go.

In the same way that physical punishment was sometimes cathartic for a submissive, he found that dominance—the routine, the ritual, the calm focus on someone else's needs, the absolute control—soothed something inside of him.

In real life, in scenes that occurred outside of the public eye, the consensual giving and accepting of pain was a big part of the draw for him, as well, but he expected none of that gratification tonight.

He eyed Julie dispassionately. She lay face-down across the spanking bench, her long brown hair caught up in a neat ponytail. She wore a halter top that exposed most of her upper back, and the type of short, loose skirt that most of the volunteers wore in demonstrations since it could be pushed up easily. He questioned Julie carefully, making sure to establish any hard limits and to ensure that she knew her safe word.

Her voice was high-pitched and she was shivering slightly, either from nerves or anticipation. Unmistakable signs that it was time for him to begin.

"I'm gonna warm you up first with my hand," he told her in a low voice. "The first set will be ten strokes. You're gonna count them off for me."

She nodded, her cheek moving against the bench, though Donnie hadn't required any further consent.

He delivered the first sharp swat to her fabric-covered ass and she jumped, just slightly.

"One," she said.

He raised his palm again, and again, and again, priming her ass, warming her flesh as she counted.

Without warning, he flipped back Julie's skirt to deliver the next set of blows, pleased to see that her skin was flushed a slight pink, when one sharp, swift gasp from the crowd snagged his attention, stole his focus.

He turned to glare at the offending observer, to deliver a silent rebuke to the gasping woman, when the unmistakable scent of cinnamon gum overwhelmed his senses.

What the fuck was Grace doing down here?

His first instinct was to stop the scene—to interrupt, exactly as he'd warned the observers *not* to do, haul Grace over his shoulder, and lock her in his apartment until she'd forgotten anything and everything she'd witnessed so far. His gaze found hers. Shock and outrage swam in her big brown eyes along with... *holy shit.* Arousal.

He felt a wash of heat roll up his back and over his shoulders. *Rage.* The woman had left his apartment, his *locked* apartment, and was strolling around The Club without a thought to who might see her, to who might *harm* her. After all he'd risked to keep her safe, after all the things they'd spoken to one another that morning.

Then Grace's eyes dropped down to his hand, which was poised to deliver another blow to Julie's ass, before meeting his again, burning in their intensity. Silently, Grace bit her lip, begging him to continue… to let her watch.

And suddenly this public demonstration became very, very personal.

He looked away, returned his gaze to Julie, where it belonged. But as he reached for the paddle, testing it against his hand while Julie trembled in front of him, a part of his consciousness was focused on one particular spectator in the crowd, one shuddering breath that caught and held as he raised the implement to strike. It wasn't Julie that he was imagining punishing, it wasn't Julie's ass that he imagined reddening with each smack of the paddle and each bite of the cane, it was the infuriating woman who had been tying him in knots for years. The smell of cinnamon overwhelmed him, and with thoughts of Grace consuming his mind, he let the paddle fly.

Chapter 4

Holy fucking hell.

Grace's heart slammed against her rib cage so hard, she feared others in the room would hear the rapid pounding. She grew so lightheaded she was barely conscious of more than a *whoosh, whoosh,* as the flames licked straight through her body and throbbed between her legs.

She'd had her fair share of dreams of Donnie, and conjured up so many fantasies that they'd become her own personal bedtime fairy tales. But never, *ever,* in a million years, had she imagined anything like the scene that played out right in front of her now. Now, as in her fantasies, he was dressed as she'd always known him—faded jeans, worn t-shirt, leather jacket, and boots. But as she watched him, she realized that her fantasies had never compensated for the way Donnie Nolan had grown up, had become a man. Though she'd seen him last night and this morning, she hadn't really *seen* him, not the *real* him.

She hadn't truly grasped the sheer breadth of him, the muscles that went from his neck and shoulders and down his back with perfect grace, evident under the thin fabric of the shirt he wore. Nor had she ever imagined him wearing all black like this, from his shirt, to his pants, to his boots, making him look dark, powerful, *amazing.* His entire body and posture commanded obedience, the very picture of authority as he stood, feet planted apart, a fucking *paddle* in his hands. She hadn't imagined the way his jaw had hardened, growing from a boy to a man, his eyes riveted now not on the woman splayed out in front of him ready to have her ass spanked, but on *Grace herself.*

"When a dom gives an instruction," he said, his deep, gritty voice carrying across the room, "he expects to be *obeyed.* And disobedience should be met with firm, *painful* consequences." His eyes bore into Grace's and though she hadn't read those eyes in years, they spoke loud and clear to her now.

He was pissed, and she was in so much fucking trouble. She swallowed, wiping her damp hands on her jeans, frozen to the spot. It was shocking, seeing him wield a paddle, and both arousing and nerve-wracking hearing his words. Suddenly, his admonition to stay safe in his apartment rang loud and clear, much clearer than it had when she had grown so restless she'd decided a bit of a walk downstairs wouldn't hurt anybody.

As his eyes narrowed on her, his hand spread across the naked lower back of the girl in front of him, and he lifted the paddle in the air.

"Firm," he said, the paddle rearing back as his gaze quickly went back to his target before he swished it through the air and brought it down with a resounding *smack* on the girl's upturned ass. The sound of the impact went straight to Grace's clit.

"Painful." Another lift and swoosh before he brought the paddle down with a second firm swat, the smack pushing the air right out of Grace's lungs.

"*Consequences.*" He punctuated his words with a final heavy swat, eyes now back on Grace.

Oh, God. There was not a doubt in her mind.

When he got her alone, he was going to spank her.

And as she shoved her thighs together, arousal zinging through her body like bolts of lightning, she realized that all these years fantasizing about Donnie, all these years slipping her fingers through her own folds in the recesses of her bed, as she imagined oh so many sweet, wicked things he'd do to her, that she'd *never* been more turned on than she was now, watching him spank *another girl*. The heat that gathered in her chest spread, vivid and painful, as both arousal and jealousy warred within her.

He stood, no longer bending over to deliver the paddling, as he exchanged the paddle for a long, thin rod.

"Canes must be used with extreme caution," he said, his voice carrying over the crowd, his focus now elsewhere. "They are not beginners' implements. Thin, supple implements like switches and canes concentrate force and are considered on the severe end of the spectrum. It's *very* easy to overdo." He was walking in a circle now, pacing as he spoke, holding the cane in one hand while tapping the other. His deep voice carried through the room, commanding the attention of everyone there like the most erudite professor. She thought of Mrs. Reynolds, that nasty hag from back in the neighborhood who used to call Donnie a punk who'd never amount to anything. She wished the bitch could see Donnie now. How could anyone accuse Donnie of being an uneducated, stupid street kid? God, he was brilliant. The crowd was riveted. As he continued, though, he came to stand in front of Grace.

"Sometimes, though, a sound punishment is necessary." His

eyes focused on hers, narrowed and *furious*. Her mouth suddenly felt as if it were stuffed with cotton. She didn't like the look of his eyes on her like that, and she squirmed as he continued. "Sometimes, a stubborn submissive needs to learn her lesson. She needs to learn to behave, and a good spanking that'll leave her sore will be a good reminder that *you mean what you say.*"

God. The breath whooshed out of her.

He turned back to the woman in front of him, once more placing a firm hand on her bare back. Grace wanted to shove that hand away, tear his fingers off the woman's flesh, and show everyone in the whole room that Donnie was *hers*.

The ferocity of her possessiveness surprised her, but she had no time to dwell as Donnie spoke again, his eyes locked on hers. "Caning is a severe punishment, and should be reserved for serious disciplinary action. In *my* book, that translates to putting yourself in danger," he said, as he lifted the cane and snapped it against the girl's bare ass with a flick of his wrist. Furious eyes, narrowed to slits, turned to her, and though the cane struck the girl on display, she knew, she could *feel*, that he wished she was the one writhing in pain under his firm grasp. "Or deliberate disobedience."

Pain. Disobedience. Punishment. Grace pushed her legs together, her heart hammering in time to the thrum of arousal that licked through her. She flinched with every soft snap of the cane, feeling his displeasure, feeling his anger, the words aimed directly at *her*. The crowd faded, and she realized Donnie had completed the caning. She was dimly aware of him introducing another dom, saying something about aftercare and that the next man would pick up the demonstration. She felt her jaw drop as Donnie stepped away, another man clad in black took his place, and the girl sprawled out on the bench turned angry eyes toward first Donnie, then her. But she had no time to understand what was happening, as Donnie was now upon her, his hand grasping her upper arm and spinning her around.

"Not one fucking word," he growled. "You say one word and I won't wait to get you upstairs before I blister your ass."

Sheer will kept her trotting to keep up with him, as her knees wobbled. She wanted to pull away from him and shield herself from his anger, since she suspected his anger hurt worse than she imagined that caning would have. If watching him spank a girl on public display made her breasts swell and her clit throb, what would it be like if the woman under his punishing palm was *her?*

Her arm felt branded by his touch, her skin aflame as he marched her along. Where were they going? She'd been going stir crazy in the room, and somehow managed to convince herself that she'd be able to watch him without him noticing her. She'd only wanted to be closer to him, only wanted to see what exactly *happened* in a BDSM club. It seemed she'd find out, all right. Had she hoped he *would* notice? She hadn't accounted for the horrible feeling that settled in the pit of her stomach now that he truly was angry with her though.

"I told you," he growled, his voice tight with anger as he marched her to privacy down a dark, narrow hallway past the main demonstration area, "to stay the *fuck* in the apartment." They were moving upstairs now, back to his place, the stairs flying by as he hauled her along with him. "Where you were *safe* and I could make sure you didn't put your *fucking life* in danger." His voice cracked, and she felt her nose tingle, her eyes filled now with tears. She'd only ever wanted to please him, even as a kid. She'd sell her soul for a mere glimpse of his beautiful brown eyes filled with pride, sign away all that she owned to see his face break out in a grin. This hurt. This *killed.*

They were at the top of the stairs now, as he fumbled with keys, but the keys were unnecessary, as she hadn't locked the door. When he realized the door was unlocked, he swore under his breath, smacked the door open, turned back to her, and hauled her through the opening.

Her heart skipped a beat as she heard the door slam and lock behind them. What would he do now? She didn't have to wait for long to find out. It seemed *he* knew *exactly* what to do now. Pulling her to where the weight bench sat in the corner of the room, he propped one boot-clad foot on the bench, and without another word, hauled her bodily over his knee. She gasped as the breath whooshed out of her, the warmth of his knee beneath her belly driving home the reality that she was about to get her ass spanked. One hand flailed helplessly in front of her, while the other instinctively flew back to block him, but he'd clearly done this a time or two. He pinned her wrist to her lower back.

This wasn't how it was supposed to go. This wasn't a sexy spanking like the ones she'd fantasized about, where she'd wiggle her hips and he'd take her over his knee, and they'd do... *something*. Not having been spanked before, she'd never known where to take the fantasy after she found herself over his lap. But wasn't he supposed to bare her, like he had the girl downstairs? She didn't want to be strewn over his knee about to get spanked like a naughty little girl, fully clothed. Her only defense now was to convince him to stop.

"Donnie, I…"

Whack! His hand cracked down on her ass, the smack echoing in the room like the blast of a canon.

Holy *shit* that hurt.

"Donnie, please!"

Whack! A second blistering smack landed. She couldn't

believe how much it hurt, even with her jeans on. Had he snagged a paddle on the way? She closed her eyes, her cheeks flaming with mortification, unable to stop him, as his hand landed over and over.

"Please what?" he growled. "Please don't spank me? Please let me put myself in danger and risk my life?" He shifted her so that her torso leaned even more precariously over his knee, her ass perched higher, another swat following another, the spanking unrelenting. This wasn't sexy. This wasn't what she'd ever imagined. She was completely, utterly embarrassed.

"No," she wailed, realizing with chagrin that her humiliation had dissolved into tears, her cheeks damp with them. With her free hand, she swiped at her eyes. "I didn't mean to. I'm sorry!" He paused while she still dangled over his knee.

"You're sorry?" Another solid *whack*. "Sorry you got caught, or sorry you're getting spanked?" *Whack!* "Sorry you scared the shit out of me?" He delivered hard, blistering swats, one right after the other, until she lost count.

"Yes," she wailed, and he finally stopped. He released her wrist, pulled her down off his knee, placed his boot on the floor, and spun her around to look at him. His huge hands grasped her shoulders and shook her, not harshly, but firmly enough to get her attention. His jaw was set, his eyes not as angry now, but probing, so serious. She watched him, the knot in her chest dissolving as she gave way to full-on sobs.

"You do what I say," he growled. "You ever fucking put yourself in danger like that again, I'll pull those pants down and spank your bare ass. Do you understand me?"

She nodded, feeling his anger, feeling how serious he was, and lifted a hand to her eyes, swiping at the tears that wouldn't stop. She wanted to run into his arms, bury her head in his chest, and cry her eyes out, but he stood apart now, released her shoulders, and placed his hands on his hips. "You get your ass in my room," he said. "Strip out of those clothes and get ready for bed." His eyes narrowed, a frown etched on his face, as he pointed one finger toward his bedroom. "*Now.*"

Grace put her head down, sniffling, and walked to his bedroom obediently. She heard him sigh, which only may her cry harder. She hated that she'd made him so angry. She felt all alone in nursing her wounds. Shuffling her feet to his bedroom, she quietly pushed open the door as she heard him on his cell phone, likely checking in to make sure everything was going as planned downstairs.

"You've got it? Thank you. Yes, sounds perfect. I'm out for the night. Tomorrow, we need to have a meeting to go over a few things. I did *not* like having it sprung on me that there was a substitute for the demo, Connie. I refuse to do another scene with Julie. Next time someone gets sick, we cancel the demo." His voice went on, but she could only focus on what he'd said. He was done for the night? He wasn't going back down?

Grace laid out the t-shirt and lounge pants he'd acquired for her, and stripped. Unfastening her jeans, she pushed them down over her hips, flinching as the sturdy fabric scraped along her sore ass. She closed her eyes as she stepped out of them, then ran her hand over the tender, punished skin. It felt warm to the touch straight through her panties. *God.* His hand was so large, and connected so firmly, she wondered if she'd be able to sit comfortably even the next day.

You ever put yourself in danger like that again, I'll pull those pants down and spank that bare ass.

She shivered, her pulse spiking in her chest as she pulled her top over her head, bunching it up, and tossing it in his laundry basket. All this time, she'd been fantasizing about getting a bare-ass spanking, and after getting a *real* spanking over jeans, she wondered if those were the types of spankings best left for fantasy. Could she *tolerate* a spanking on bare skin from Donnie?

Hiccupping, she stepped into the pants. She'd have to brush her teeth and wash up, but she was in no mood to see Donnie right now. All she wanted to do was crawl under the covers and pull them up over her head. She laid down on his bed, the pile of pillows below her cheek offering little consolation. As her tears slowed, she replayed the scene in her mind. Somehow, she'd imagined being spanked by Donnie would've been a whole lot hotter and a lot less mortifying than it actually was.

As she thought about it, she realized he hadn't been amiss. She'd disobeyed his instruction to stay safe and out of reach of those outside his barrier of protection. She wasn't supposed to leave the apartment without him. Though at the time, she'd thought her plan to quietly observe downstairs would be fine, she realized now how vulnerable she'd made herself. She had no idea where the exits were, what video cameras were set up, or who would be downstairs.

She'd been stupid, and she'd paid the price. She closed her eyes, suddenly feeling very, very alone, rejected even. Was he still angry with her? She hated the idea of him being angry with her. Where did this leave them? The craziness of her question made her almost laugh. She didn't know when she'd be able to return to her home, or go back to work, or if she or her brother would make it out of this whole fiasco alive, and her biggest concern at the moment was how Donnie would forgive her. And *why* had he treated her like a little girl? That hadn't been a sexy spanking, like he'd given the gorgeous girl in the demo. That had been purely to punish her, damn it. Was she still just a little girl to him?

The door creaked, and her eyes flew open. He stood in the doorway, the dim light from the living room casting him in shadow. He'd stripped out of his black top and stood in a white t-shirt, and jeans, his hands tucked into his pockets as he leaned against the door frame. His hair hung loose about his face, longish and tousled, like he'd just gotten off his bike.

Suddenly self-conscious, she turned away and pulled the covers up to hide her face, acutely aware of her scorched ass.

He'd *spanked* her. God in heaven, he'd taken her over his knee and spanked her. She swallowed, another lump rising in her throat just looking at him.

His voice was soft when he spoke. "You okay, honey?"

He couldn't be all sweet and tender, not now, when she was nursing her wounds and still trying to figure out what the hell had just happened. Yeah, she was *fine*. She'd swallow her tears and tell him she was *fine, thank you*. But the moment she opened her mouth, it seemed she no longer had any control over what she said or how she reacted.

He'd spanked her like a naughty little girl.

"No," she whispered, her tears starting afresh. Hell no, she wasn't okay. Her chin wobbled and her voice cracked. "I'm not okay." She turned her back to him, buried her face in the pillow, and stifled her cries. Her lack of control embarrassed her, but she couldn't seem to get a grip. "Just go away," she mumbled into the pillow, but the little voice inside her head pleaded, *please don't go*.

She heard a creak, as she felt the bed sag. Was he sitting on the edge? But no, a moment later she was lifted bodily up into his long, strong, capable arms, and he was cradling her against his chest as he sat on the bed. "Grace," he said, his voice husky and filled with emotion. "Come here, angel."

The term of endearment broke her will further, and she

sobbed against his chest. He held her silently, hushing her as he rocked her in his arms. She cried for oh so many things. For her mama, as she imagined her pacing the house, worrying about her daughter. She cried for Pedro, who was a certifiable asshole, but who was her *brother.* But most of all, she cried because she'd let down her knight in shining armor, her *hero.*

"Grace," he said softly, softer than she'd ever heard him speak. He kissed the top of her head and slowly rocked her until her sobs quieted. "You had a lot you were holding onto, didn't you?" he asked, and she nodded.

Her nose was stuffed and her eyes swollen as she looked up at him. "For some reason, when I thought about you sp-spanking me, I always thought it would be a lot hotter than it was in reality." A day or two earlier, admitting she fantasized about him spanking her would have embarrassed her, but now, it seemed everything was laid bare, and there was no reason to hold back.

He laughed, holding her tighter to his chest. "You've thought about it before?"

She nodded. "Um, yeah."

His chuckles quieted. "It *can* be hot, honey," he said, "and someday, I'll show you exactly what a sexy spanking is like." He paused, as if he suddenly became aware of her body pressed up against his, and what he'd just said. Her cheek pressed against his dampened shirt, and as she lay in his arms listening to his heartbeat, she felt him beneath her... not just his legs or his arms, but his hardened length. She turned him on. God, *she turned him on.* She lifted her face off his chest, needing to see his eyes, and when she did, she gasped, as his mouth met hers. He kissed her the way she'd always hoped he would, like he wanted to mark her as his own, their lips crushed together in a mingling of salty tears and sultry tongues, his hands raking up her top and kneading her breasts.

He pulled his mouth off hers just long enough to whisper, "That spanking wasn't sexy for you, angel? That punishment didn't make you wet for me, even a *little?*" Oh *God*, when he put it *that* way, she felt her thighs clench together as his hand went to her waist and pulled the drawstring. "You sure?" The mere sound of his voice made her nipples harden, but the warmth of his fingers on her belly made her gasp.

"No," she breathed. "Not sexy. Not. *Sexy!*"

The very tip of his finger was at the top of her panties now, tugging on the elastic waistband. Oh, God, *yes*.

"You're not even a *little* turned on?"

She held onto his arms as he gently stroked her. His deep, rumbling laugh made her cheeks blush. "Not sexy, huh? Then why are you so wet for me?"

"Because it's *you*," she said before she could help herself. Maybe she was in denial. Maybe it *had* been sexy? Because now that his finger was *there*, moving with skill through her most sensitive parts, she realized just how very aroused she actually was. Just a few more touches and she'd come undone, right here over his lap, her throbbing ass against his erection, while his breath tickled her cheek and Donnie took control over her body. To her shock, he pulled his hand away, and gently pushed her so that he could hold her at arm's length, her panties snapping back.

His lips thinned as he shook his head sadly. "So soon after being punished, Grace?" he asked. His eyes had grown serious. "I thought you learned your lesson."

What?

He lifted her and turned her torso, flipping her over his lap. She pushed against him, wanting to know what the hell he was playing at, but she was no match for him. He chuckled, holding her straight over his knees, her belly against his warm thighs, her fingers grasping onto his legs. "Uh uh, angel."

"Donn*ieee*," she wailed. He wasn't going to… spank her again? Was he? Why else would he pull her belly-down over his lap?

His large, warm hand rested on her aching backside. His voice was a deep rumble as he spoke again. "Did you lie to me *again*, Grace? I let it go once, but do you think I'll let it go again?"

"No!" she protested. But, well, maybe she had. She hadn't exactly told him the whole truth of what she knew, had she? "Well…" she faltered, "I… maybe I…" Her voice trailed off.

"Now, now, Grace," he scolded. "You already know what happens when you misbehave. Do you think I like when you lie to me?" She felt his finger on the edge of her panties, drawing them down slowly over her ass. She squirmed, warmth seeping through her, so turned on it wasn't even funny. Unhurriedly, he dragged the thin fabric down her thighs, the heat of his fingers branding her as he slowly, *so* slowly, pulled her panties to her ankles. Then she felt his hand drift between her legs, spreading them apart, and one wicked finger was between her folds. He continued to admonish her. "What happens when you defy me, angel?"

She closed her eyes as her head swam with arousal. Her mouth felt dry, and she forgot how to speak. To her shock, his hand came down in a sharp swat that made her gasp and arch her back, before he spoke again. "I asked you a question, Grace, and I expect an answer."

"I-I get spanked when I disobey you!"

He growled his approval. "Damn right," he said, with another sharp but not altogether unpleasant smack. It was hard enough she could feel it, but light enough that it was hardly unbearable. He continued spanking her with firm but sensual smacks, the warmth spreading over her naked skin. Pausing, his fingers explored her folds, and he made a tsking sound of disapproval when he found her wet for him.

"Your body betrays you, angel," he said with a dark chuckle. "You told me getting spanked by me wasn't sexy." The very tip of his finger circled her clit, making her arch her back in pleasure. He bent his head, his whiskered chin grazing her cheek before the deep rumble of his whisper tickled her ear. "Do you need a spanking, Grace? Do I need to punish you for lying?"

And something clicked. She needed *more*. She needed him to make her come. Arching her back, squirming against his touch to encourage him to touch her again, she moaned. "I've been so bad," she whispered. "You're right. I need a sp-spanking." Her cheeks flamed saying it, but he knew how to handle her.

He gave her two more stinging swats, but this time, her clit throbbed with each stroke of his hand, and then his fingers were in her, pumping in her core, before gliding deliciously through her arousal. She was going to lose it. She was going to come right here, over his lap, after being spanked. Grasping his leg, she wriggled, so close now she could taste it, on the cusp of losing control.

His voice no longer teased. "Push that pretty little cunt against my hand," he demanded. She felt one hand swirl through her hair, and with a firm, deliberate tug, her head pulled back. Oh *God*. Who knew getting her hair pulled like this would be so sexy? She closed her eyes. God! "Take it, angel," he ordered, two fingers expertly stroking her while he tugged her hair again, a sharp but sensual ache she felt all the way down her spine. "That's it, Grace. That's my sweet little slut."

Holy *hell*, she loved this. Donnie Nolan was pulling her hair and spanking her ass, his fingers doing wicked things while he called her his slut. *Yes. She wanted this.* She was about to fly out of her fucking *skin* as he growled, insisting, "Come for me, baby. Fucking *come.*" This time, she obeyed, shock waves riding her body to ecstasy. She gasped and writhed as he stroked her. "Yeah, just like that. God, yeah, angel." He continued to fondle and tease her as she rode her orgasm, whispering dirty, wicked things in her ear, until she lay, spent, over his lap.

Her body felt limp, every emotion rent from her, as she lay unmoving.

He caressed her back, his rough but gentle touch moving down to her aching ass, soothing the pain, his touch bringing home how pleased he was with her, how very much he cared.

"That's a good girl," he whispered. "Time for bed, now, Grace." She already felt half asleep. He turned her over and cradled her in his arms, holding her against his chest while he lay back on the pillows. Reaching for the covers, he pulled them up over her, tucking them up against her while he held her. She fell asleep like that, too tired to even understand what had just happened but too happy to care.

"Morning, sunshine." Donnie sat on the edge of the bed with a cup of coffee.

Grace sat up. What time was it? Her eyes felt bleary, and her head fuzzy, reminding her of her need for coffee.

"Seems the nighttime festivities wore you out," he said with a chuckle, handing her a mug. She took a tentative sip and sighed.

Delicious. Creamy, sweet, the rich breakfast blend she'd come to appreciate.

Looking away shyly, Grace nodded. Uh, yeah, getting hauled over his knee and soundly spanked, then brought to climax while he punished her in the most delicious of ways? Those nighttime festivities had worn her the hell out all right.

"You drink your coffee and listen up, babe. We've gotta talk about a few things." Though he was nowhere as stern as he'd been the night before, his tone was serious, and to her surprise, she felt immediately willing to do what he said. Had the spanking the night before changed something?

She sipped her coffee, nodding, as he continued. "I've got shit to do today. You're gonna call your mom, and I'll help you come up with a story that will keep her content for now. We still have some time before Mikey's guys realize you're gone, and I've got some guys looking into the situation. I'm gonna meet with them later and work out a plan. Yeah?"

"Yeah, I guess," she said, putting her mug down. "What am I going to do about work? You know I don't want to run away, Donnie."

His lips turned down in a frown, and his brow furrowed. "I'll take care of this," he said sternly. "Don't start giving me lip, Grace."

She squirmed on her still-throbbing backside. Nope, she wasn't gonna give him lip.

"Already took care of your work," he said, taking a long pull from his own mug.

She frowned. "What do you mean?"

"Had a word with your manager."

She blinked. "You... did?"

Her manager was a power-hungry, middle-aged woman

who'd been working retail since before Grace was even born. She clocked her employees the second they stepped in the door, and had a timer in the breakroom that she set when they took their breaks, an obnoxious fluorescent contraption suitable for keeping time at a basketball game. Her face was set in a perpetual frown, and Grace was fairly certain that she absolutely hated Grace's guts.

"What'd she say?" Grace asked warily.

He shrugged. "Take all the time you need," he said.

Okay. Scratch that. "What'd *you* say?" she asked, shaking her head, absolutely bemused.

He grinned, one of those rare, panty-melting grins that made her heart forget how to keep a steady beat. "You let me worry about that, babe. I may have given her an ample tip to keep quiet."

Well, then. Grace couldn't help but laugh.

"Today, you'll stay here while I have shit to do," he said. "You can use my iPad, workout equipment, whatever you need. I got some books from Hillary loaded on the iPad. She's one of my friends' wives, and she writes those shit romance books you girls like. They sell really well, so maybe they're good." His lips pursed. "I wouldn't know."

Grace snorted. She hadn't cracked open a romance novel in her entire life, but she'd give it a go. Sure beat staring at his walls.

"If you're good," he said, his brows pulling together as he sobered, "and by *good*, I mean you don't move a fucking toe out of this apartment, then tonight I'll order takeout and we'll watch a movie or something. What do you think?"

Her heart soared. Her entire life was in disarray. She had no idea how she'd get out of this mess or what her future held. But right now, right here, as she sat in his bed and stared at him with what she knew to be starry-eyed adoration, she could only nod. "Yeah," she breathed, burying her face in her coffee cup for another sip to swallow against the ridiculous surge of excitement she felt.

He nodded, once, and placed his cup down on the bedside table. "Grace?" he asked, all trace of teasing gone now as he eyed her long and hard.

"Mmhmm?" she said, looking at him shyly.

"I mean it, babe," he said, his voice getting that low, grumbly sound she knew well. She nodded, as he continued. "I have *serious* shit to do today. I cannot monitor your every move. I need to trust that you're not gonna leave this place. This is where you're safe. You get me?"

"Yeah," she said. "I get you."

"Good," he said, with a nod, as his brown eyes pierced her and his jaw set. "Because you know exactly what will happen if you leave." He paused, letting his words sink in. "*Don't* you?"

She nodded. "Uh huh."

He narrowed his eyes, his arms crossing on his chest. "Tell me, then, angel. What happens if you leave this apartment?"

God! He wanted her to say it? She looked away and couldn't meet his eyes, but her response wasn't good enough for him. He leaned over, grasping the back of her hair and pulling her head back. Shit, that was sexy and scary all at once. She swallowed, her eyes shifting to his.

"Tell me," he growled. "Tell me what happens if you leave this apartment. I want you to say the fucking words."

"You'll punish me," she said in a rush of words, her pulse spiking.

He tugged her hair again. "You leave this apartment today,

after what happened last night, and I swear to God I'll take my belt to your ass. You get me?"

She nodded. Satisfied with her answer, he released her. She got him all right. What she didn't get was how she could be scared, chastened, and turned on all at the very same time. She had no idea what tomorrow would bring, or how she'd get out of her predicament, but there was one thing she knew for sure. Things would never be the same again.

Chapter 5

"So... you took her from your brother's house and brought her to The Club?"

Blake's voice on the phone carried the deceptively mild tone he often used when he was pissed off, and the hand Donnie had braced against the casing of his office window clenched into a fist. He'd told Blake everything that had happened in the past two days, barring any of the events that had occurred after the demo last night, of course, and had admitted he needed Blake's help. He owed Blake huge, and never wanted the man to regret taking a chance on him all those years ago, but this was Grace's *life* he was talking about here. Pride had no place in this conversation.

"Yeah, boss. I did. It's the safest place," Donnie confirmed, repeating words he'd spoken earlier.

"Uh huh. So you said. I'm just wondering why you trusted Slay's guy Lucas to take charge of the brother, who's fucked six ways to Sunday, incidentally, since he knows where all of your cousin Mikey's bodies are buried, *literally*. But you wouldn't trust Lucas to find a safe house for Grace."

Donnie gripped his phone tightly, watching the sun glinting off the cars parked outside, and fought to keep his breathing even. He knew what Blake was seeing here, what he wanted Donnie to admit. The man wasn't wrong. But Donnie hadn't had a chance to untangle his own complicated feelings about the woman who was currently upstairs sleeping in his apartment. He was in no place to have this conversation with Blake.

"Figured it was better to keep 'em separate," Donnie hedged, turning away from the window and throwing himself into his desk chair. "Besides which, Grace isn't exactly a willing guest here. The woman has zero sense of self-preservation. She refuses to leave town, and I've already had to threaten *multiple times* to tan her ass if she leaves my apartment without permission."

He hadn't realized that his voice had become a low growl until Blake spoke again.

"You've threatened multiple times?" the man repeated. "Huh. You must be losing your touch, *Master Nolan*." His voice was tinged with amusement now, and for some reason that grated on Donnie even more than the annoyed, mild voice had.

"That's because Grace isn't my *submissive*," Donnie returned, trying to ignore the fact that he'd lectured her, spanked her hard, and brought her to orgasm mere hours ago. *If it walks like a duck and quacks like a duck...*

He grabbed a pen and began tapping it on his desk, then recognized the nervous habit for what it was and immediately threw the pen back down in disgust.

"Hmm," was Blake's reply. Then he cleared his throat. "Well, in any case, we've got a situation to deal with here. I'll assemble the troops."

Relief made a knot unclench in Donnie's gut. He'd expected no less from Blake, knowing the man as he did, though the fact that Blake would always have his back was something Donnie never took for granted. Still, he knew Blake was *not* happy with the situation.

"I need you to know, boss, that I woulda never brought her here if I thought it endangered The Club. This place is my priority, and I—"

"Don," Blake interrupted. "I know. I trust you. My concern over this situation has nothing to do with The Club, or even with your Grace."

Donnie frowned. "All right."

"I'm worried about you," Blake continued. "You're not just my employee, you *know* that. Elena and I consider you family. Your cousin is bad news and I can't say I'm excited that you've been dragged back into his shit. But I respect that you did what you felt you had to do. Now the guys and I are gonna help you. Right?"

"Right," Donnie said gruffly. "Thanks, man. So you and the guys will come here tonight?" Blake knew the Club South was closed that evening, and would provide the perfect cover for a meet. Plus, it ensured that Donnie could stick close to Grace.

"No," Blake shocked the hell out of him by saying. "Not there. I'll call Tony. I bet we can have the back room at *Cara*."

Cara was the Italian restaurant that Donnie's friend Tony, who also happened to be his boss Matteo's younger brother, owned in the North End of Boston… miles away from The Club South.

"Boss, I really don't feel comfortable leaving Grace…" Donnie said.

"Hell no," Blake agreed. "Bring her with you. I'll bring Elena, and I'll see if the other guys wanna bring their wives, make it a family thing."

A family thing... Because Blake's crew: Dom, Matt, Tony, Slay, Paul, and the rest, along with their families, had somehow morphed into the world's weirdest, *best* family.

Something warm and pleasant unfurled in Donnie's chest, even as he forced himself to say, "Do you think it's safe, dragging them into this?"

"You said your brother is covering for Grace, and you trust him to do that because he owes you. Mikey won't even know she's missing for another half a week, and would have no immediate idea that *you* were involved even if he did. True?"

"Yeah," Donnie agreed reluctantly.

"Plus, Don, recall that our friends are a lot better trained and a fuck of a lot better *connected* than your average group of guys." Blake's voice was amused.

Donnie snorted. Matteo and Slay were retired Marines who still did security and investigative work, Blake himself was a former soldier... and there wasn't a single one of those men Donnie wouldn't want beside him in a fight.

"Right," he admitted.

"Right," Blake repeated. "I'll report all of this to the guys, let them make their own decisions. But that girl is gonna need some support, Don. If she's been living under Mikey's thumb for years like you said, making some friends in the *outside world* is imperative. And there are no better women than this bunch."

Donnie sighed. Blake was right, but the knowledge that Grace needed other people rankled on some level. Donnie liked the idea of Grace relying on *him*... maybe a little too much. He knew that once this was over and Grace was safe, their time together at The Club would be over. Grace would move on to choose her own future, and live the life she should have had; Donnie would insist on it. And she couldn't ask for better friends to help her with that than the wives and partners of Blake's crew.

Donnie and Blake agreed on a time, then Donnie ended the call, throwing his phone down next to his laptop. God, he was fucking exhausted.

Already this morning, he'd had to deal with Julie's sudden appearance, approximately twelve hours *before* her scheduled shift, bringing donuts and coffee for the construction workers and a flirtatious smile for Donnie. That smile had killed any hope Donnie had entertained that Julie might not have read too much into his overly-enthusiastic demonstration last night. And, in truth, Donnie couldn't totally blame her. He'd brought this on himself. Yeah, he'd *told her* he wanted nothing beyond a business relationship, but the spanking he'd delivered last night had been far more passionate than the distant, clinical demonstrations he normally delivered, and there was no doubt Julie had noticed. Julie had no idea that he'd been fantasizing about having *Grace* splayed out on that spanking bench, that he'd imagined *Grace's* ass at his mercy. He'd have to quadruple his efforts to keep his distance from Julie now, or talk to Blake about reassigning her to The Club's Boston location.

Donnie turned his chair around and looked at the window again, letting his mind go blank and the tension bleed from his shoulders for just a minute. He ran his hand through his hair, idly wondering if he should get it cut. It was getting long now, a little longer than he preferred, but it sure as hell seemed like Grace liked it just the way it was.

God. He recognized the direction of his thoughts, and annoyance flared before he shut it down.

Did Grace like his *hair*? Would *she* want him to get it cut? Next he'd be asking her if she agreed with the plans for renovating the third floor, or where she thought he should go the next time he took his bike out for the day. Since when had Grace's opinions factored into his decision-making? But an insistent little voice in the back of his head had the answer to that.

Always.

And that's why it bugged the hell out of him, if he were being honest. He'd created a life for himself. Hell, he'd had to fucking *carve* that life out of solid granite with nothing but his own two hands, but he'd done it. He'd had less than nothing when he walked away from Mikey; no money, no home, no friends, no skills except for fighting. It would have been easy, back then, to keep doing what he'd been doing: to find a place in another crew like Mikey's, to keep breaking legs and shaking people down, to maybe find comfort in the bottle the way his old man had. But Donnie hadn't even considered it.

Instead, he'd answered an ad in the paper that had led him to Blake. He'd told the man he wasn't afraid to learn or to work hard, and with Blake's help, he'd done both. He'd gotten himself to a place where he was content and independent. He had money now, thousands in the bank, thanks in part to the guys letting him live at The Club South for free. He had a place where he belonged, and skills as a dominant and a business manager that were unique and valued. He had friends, *good ones*, who accepted him as he was and made him want to be an even better man. And this whole time, as he'd carved out this life, he'd thought his underlying purpose had been to become a man that he could be proud of.

But now he realized it hadn't been his *own* standards he was trying to live up to, they'd been Grace's. She'd been only thirteen when he'd left her. A *kid* for God's sake. But she'd still been the best person with the purest heart he'd ever encountered.

He'd wanted to be someone *she* could be proud of.

And now she was back in his life. Not as a ghost or as a memory, but as a flesh and blood woman with needs and desires and... and... fuck. *Expectations*. Grace deserved a man who would wear a suit and work a nine-to-five, then return to their suburban house each night and cook dinner while she worked on her art or played with their two-point-five children. She deserved a man who liked driving a sedan, and whose idea of kink was taking her to see that silly movie about the billionaire dominant, after she'd pestered and teased him into going. She deserved that life, one that was normal and wholesome.

She deserved better than to be corrupted by a sadist who had only learned to restrain his sexual impulses thanks to the ruthless control and discipline he'd discovered when training as a dominant. She deserved more than a man whose life's plan involved one day getting on his bike and not stopping until he'd found a place that called to him, and declaring that *home*.

Grace had been waiting for sex, saving herself, for twenty-five years. She deserved better than the likes of him.

The air was warm for late May, and the smell of the damp earth and the rotting garbage in the nearby cans assaulted his senses, but his makeshift bed on the old picnic table in the Diazes' backyard was too comfortable for him to bother moving.

He peered up at the dark sky, looking for the North Star, but there was nothing up there but unrelenting black. The fucking thing should be up there somewhere, shouldn't it? Figured the damn thing showed itself to everyone but him.

He shifted his head for a better look, feeling his stomach lurch in response to the movement.

Okay, so maybe his comfort right now came less from the picnic table and more from the half bottle of Jameson's he'd guzzled before hopping the chain-link fence into the yard. Either way, he'd take what comfort he could get.

The bright flash of headlights turning down the side street hit him full in the eyes and made him wince, which in turn made pain flare across his injured cheek and down the jaw.

Shit, that hurt.

Carmichael had put up a fight. Didn't that asshole know things would only go worse for him if he fought back? Donnie himself had learned that lesson at age seven, courtesy of his father, but apparently some people took longer to get the message.

He lifted his right hand into the air slowly, trying to make out its shape in the darkness, before curling his bruised and swollen knuckles into a fist.

Whelp. Motherfucker had learned the lesson real good this time, hadn't he? Education courtesy of the talented Professor Nolan, who would never have his high school diploma, but had a fucking PhD in assault.

Donnie blew out a tired breath and felt a sickness surge in his belly that had nothing to do with the alcohol or his injuries. He was nineteen, but on nights like this, he felt like he was ninety.

The sound of a car door slamming brought him back to reality. He swung his legs off the table and brought his feet to rest on the attached bench seat, slowly lifting himself up to a seated position.

It was harder than he'd anticipated.

He needed to get himself back to Joe's house. Maybe Karen would take pity on him and mop up the dents on his face like she sometimes did. He didn't know why he'd come over here in the first place. Last thing he needed was for Papa Diaz to catch him on the property, especially now that he blamed Donnie for encouraging Pedro to join the Nolan family business.

Like Pedro had needed any encouragement.

A new sound came through the darkness, soft and heartbreaking. Someone was... crying?

"*Grace?*" *He whispered her name instinctively, and the crying immediately cut off.*

"*D-donnie?*"

Shit. It was *Grace. He could barely see the outline of her as she rose from the back stoop and stared out into the dark yard, looking for him.*

"*Over here,*" *he said, a little louder.* "*On the picnic table.*" *His head throbbed, but adrenaline had started churning through him, burning off the worst of the alcohol. Why was Grace upset? Who the fuck had made Grace cry?*

"*Donnie, what are you doing here?*" *she asked, pausing maybe a foot away from the table, as though afraid to get too close.*

Was she scared of him now? He felt that same sick feeling he'd felt earlier rise up to choke him.

"*Honey, why are you crying?*" *he demanded, ignoring her question. He held out a hand to her, praying she'd see it and step closer, praying that she wouldn't run away.*

She inhaled a shuddering breath and took that step, and then another, until she was close enough to touch. The relief he felt was overwhelmed by something sharper and stronger as she knelt between his spread knees on the bench seat and leaned up to bury her face in his chest and wrap her arms around his waist.

He inhaled sharply. Cinnamon sugar and Grace.

Something shifted inside him, and without conscious thought, his left hand came up to wrap around her back while his injured right hand stroked her pretty hair soothingly.

"*Tell me,*" *he said firmly.* "*What happened?*"

"*I was so stupid,*" *she sobbed.* "*Tyler Kisk asked me to the eighth grade dance. And I said yes. But I don't like him.*"

"*You don't?*" *Donnie began to suspect that maybe he'd had too much to drink, since Grace's logic made his head whirl.*

"*I mean, I don't like him in a* boyfriend *way,*" *she clarified.* "*Until tonight I thought he was an okay guy, you know? It's just, I've had a crush on this, um… other *boy,* for forever. And I know it's not gonna go anywhere, at least not until I'm older. But I thought if I had more experience and dated other guys, maybe this other *boy,* would see that I'm not a kid anymore. So I told Tyler yes, and then… I couldn't do it."

"Couldn't go with him?" Donnie guessed, trying to ignore the way Grace's eyes darted to him when she spoke of this other *boy,* and the way it made his heart race, even though he knew it shouldn't.

"No! I went with him. But then he tried to kiss me."

"Did he now?" Donnie's soft voice sounded threatening even to his own ears, and he just didn't care. "And what happened?"

"I… I wanted to let him," she told him miserably. "I was going to let him. But then, when he tried, I just couldn't! He wasn't the boy I really like." She swallowed, then continued. "He didn't like it when I said no."

If some punk had hurt her… Donnie squeezed his eyes shut and welcomed the pain that flared across his face as he did so, struggling to control his temper.

"Explain," he snapped.

She sniffed loudly and tried to compose herself. "He called me a tease. He said that normal girls liked kissing and… sex. And that I was messed up if I didn't."

Fuck. He squeezed his sore hand shut and remained silent, trying to remind himself why killing thirteen-year-old shitheads was not okay.

Grace lifted her head and looked at him. The night was black and still, but somehow her eyes still shone. "Is he right?" she whispered.

"No. Hell no." His denial was immediate and instinctive.

She nodded. "I thought so. I mean, sex… making love… it should mean something, right? It should be special."

Donnie licked his lips. "Yeah. It should."

"So… have you ever?" she began.

"Ah, hell, Grace…" Of course he fucking had. Mikey had gotten him a *girl to celebrate his manhood when he was... Jesus. He'd been Grace's age. And Lord knew, he hadn't lived like a monk since, either.*

He blew out a breath. "Don't go by what I've done, honey. You set your sights higher, you hear me? You're so fucking special, Grace. You wait for that special person. Be true to yourself. And don't ever let anyone convince you to do something you don't wanna do."

Grace nodded, and the strands of her smooth hair slipped and slid beneath his hands. She gazed up at him trustingly, the one person who'd always believed in him, the one person he'd always believed in.

He hadn't realized that he'd leaned down until he felt her breath, warm and sweet against his lips. Later, he'd try to blame it on the Jameson's... on the dark night... on his fucked up mental state... on her beautiful eyes... but when she leaned up and pressed her mouth chastely against his, he let her.

This, *something inside him whispered.* This is why you came here tonight.

Somewhere nearby, a dog barked. A light in the neighbor's yard went on, bathing the yard with a yellow glow, and the moment was shattered. Grace opened her eyes, Donnie shifted his head back like he'd been electrocuted, and they got their first clear look at one another.

Grace wore a pretty dress and sweater, her hair clipped back with a flower barrette. She looked beautiful... and so damn innocent. Suddenly, he realized that his hands were on her, sliding down her hair. Those same broken, battered hands that had committed violence tonight. He moved them away from her as though they were singed.

But Grace didn't seem to notice. Her attention was focused on his face, which throbbed with each panicked beat of his heart. Her eyes widened and her mouth dropped open.

"Donnie! Oh my God! What happened to you? Who did this?"

She looked horrified, sickened. She reached her hand up to touch his busted cheek, but he turned away and wouldn't let her.

"Nobody."

"It wasn't nobody! Donnie, you need to go to the police! You need to tell someone! You..."

He shut his eyes as if that could block out her words. Never had the divide between them been more clear to him. Grace lived in a world where people called the police when they'd been the victim of assault. Donnie... was the thug who did the assaulting.

He pushed her away roughly and stood.

"Forget this, Grace," he told her.

She shook her head.

"Yes!" he demanded, grabbing her shoulders and shaking her gently. "I want you to go upstairs right now and forget I was ever here. Forget any of this happened. You hear me?"

He didn't wait for her to answer. He turned away, vaulting the short fence with an ease that belied the amount of alcohol he'd consumed and the whirl of emotions going through his brain.

But as his feet hit the street, he was almost sure he heard her whisper, "I will never forget you, Donnie."

Or maybe that was his own wishful thinking.

"Don? Hey, have you had any of these little spinach things? They're amazing."

Elena's hand was a warm weight on his shoulder and Donnie looked up, distracted from his thoughts. Ghosts and memories he'd held back for over a decade were fucking with his mind today, and he'd somehow spent the entire afternoon remembering the way Grace's lips had felt on his all those years ago... and how his hand had felt on her ass last night.

He glanced at the woman in question, watching as she chatted politely with Tony's sister-in-law Nora, Dom's wife Heidi, and Heidi's business partner Paul, on the other side of the room, near a table set with hors d'oeuvres. Despite his distraction, there hadn't been a single moment tonight when he hadn't been viscerally aware of Grace's position in the room, keeping tabs on her safety as well as her mood.

She'd been nervous as hell when he'd told her the plan for the night, though she'd tried to hide it. She'd peppered him with a million questions about the people she'd be meeting—his bosses and their wives and friends—and he'd reassured her that she looked beautiful, and the jeans and sweater she was wearing were perfectly appropriate for this group. He'd thought she'd calmed down a bit after that. She'd enjoyed the ride over, gripping his waist tight but without fear, just as she had the other night. But he'd felt her growing tension when they'd pulled off the highway and he'd started maneuvering the bike down the narrow streets near the restaurant. When he'd parked the bike, she'd hesitated before swinging her leg over the seat, like she wanted to stay on the bike forever. He didn't blame her.

But Christ, the woman was strong. She'd dropped his hand the moment he'd helped her dismount, squared her shoulders, and walked bravely by his side into *Cara*, meeting all of his friends with her smile firmly in place. She'd been eager to hear about everyone's kids, all but the littlest of whom were safely at home with babysitters tonight, and charmed all of them with her sweetness and genuine interest in getting to know them. It had seemed so important to her to stand on her own two feet and not hide behind him, that although it went against all his protective instincts, he'd let her. He'd bet he was the only one who guessed that she'd felt uncomfortable. Damn, but he was proud of her.

"Donnie?" Elena repeated.

He brought his gaze to Elena's face, and saw that she was

smirking as she placed a small plate of hors d'oeuvres on the enormous rectangular table in front of him. "Eat the spinach things, honey. I swear, she won't disappear while you're chewing."

Donnie rolled his eyes. "Thanks. You've got this honorary bossy big sister thing down, huh?"

Elena smiled. "I was sure you were gonna say it was a *mom* thing, and I am *way* too young to be your mother." She sank into the chair next to him and stretched out her legs with a groan.

It was Donnie's turn to smirk this time. "You sure about that? You're creaking like an old lady."

Elena raised an eyebrow at him. "*You* try being up all night with a teething eight-month-old, chaperoning your toddler's daycare field trip to the Children's Museum, then working a full afternoon at the office."

Donnie nodded. He knew that was just the tip of the iceberg of what Elena did, and that her afternoon at "the office," meant hours spent at *Centered*, the women's health clinic where she did everything from counseling patients as a nurse, to fundraising and budget preparation in the back office.

Still, he wouldn't be her honorary brother if he didn't give her a ration of shit.

"That's a lot for a woman of your advanced years," he deadpanned.

Elena narrowed her eyes and shook her head at him in outrage, just as Blake approached carrying their infant daughter and a glass of seltzer. He handed Elena the glass, and she took it gratefully.

"Thanks, baby. It's good to know that *some* men have manners," she told her husband, before looking pointedly at Donnie's plate. "Eat your damn spinach thing, ingrate, or I will."

Her Hero

Donnie rolled his eyes again and grinned as he obediently stuffed one of the spinach things in his mouth.

Damn. They *were* amazing.

"You teasing my wife again, Don?" Blake asked, rubbing a hand over the sleeping baby's back.

Donnie smiled and shrugged, but didn't answer. From the corner of his eye, he saw Grace and the others making their way towards the table.

"Aw! Is Donnie being mean to you, Elena?" Slay teased, scooting into the chair two seats down from Donnie, and pulling his petite, blonde wife Allie to sit on his far side.

Elena rolled her eyes at the muscle-bound giant who actually *was* her big brother, and smiled at Grace, who had stopped next to Donnie's chair. Donnie pulled out the chair between him and Slay, gestured for Grace to sit down.

"I think these two tag-team," Elena told Grace dryly. "My real brother, and my honorary one. Pretty sure they get together and think up ways to drive me insane."

"To be fair, Elena," Slay said with a grin. "It's not a far drive, is it?"

Allie burst into laughter, and Donnie almost choked on his spinach puff. Donnie saw Grace blink in surprise at the teasing before hiding her grin behind her hand, not wanting to offend Elena.

Elena laughed and put up her hands in surrender. "Enough. *God.* I have two children of my own to manage, I can't handle the two of you, too."

"I feel your pain, Elena," Dom said, taking a seat on the opposite side of the table, next to his wife, Heidi. His face was serious, but his eyes were twinkling. "It's hard being the polite sibling, isn't it?"

From his seat on the other side of Allie, Dom's twin Matteo scoffed. "*You* were never the polite one of the three of us. That was Tony."

"*What* was Tony?" Tony asked, coming to the table with a huge platter of something that smelled delicious.

"The kiss-ass, polite Angelico brother," Matteo answered, leaning over to inspect the platter and groaning appreciatively. "That chicken parm?"

"Why yes, indeed it *is*, Matt," Tony informed him with overstated politeness, as Tess, who was very pregnant, set down an enormous bowl of pasta next to the chicken. "And *someone* had to make up for the two of you. Matteo was out playing football and chasing cheerleaders, and Dom spent all his free time up in his bedroom pretending to read while actually plotting world domination or some shit. *One* of us had to wear the halo, Grace." He heaved a long-suffering sigh and shot Grace a quick smile.

"And it's such an *attractive* halo, honey," Tess said, kissing Tony's cheek affectionately, while Matteo made a gagging noise and Nora giggled.

"You know, I can totally see that scenario," Heidi said seriously. "To this day, my husband plots domination… just on a slightly smaller scale."

"Somebody's gotta do it, babe," Paul said, pulling out the chair next to Heidi's and giving Dom an appreciative fist-bump before he sat down.

"Wait, what did I miss?" Paul's boyfriend John asked, setting garlic bread and salad on the table before taking his seat next to Paul. "Who's gotta do what?"

"Somebody's gotta *plot domination*," Hillary scoffed, rolling her eyes across the table at John.

John blinked. "You all plot it, huh? Figures. And here I thought you all just made it up as you went along."

Paul snorted and laid his arm across the back of John's chair.

Grace sidled her chair closer to Donnie's and he instinctively leaned toward her.

"Are you *all*... you know?" she asked softly.

"Dominants and submissives?" he whispered back.

She nodded, a blush staining her cheeks.

"Yup. All different flavors, and the dynamic functions differently for each of us, but... essentially? Yeah."

Grace nodded again, looking around the table. He could practically hear the gears whirling around in her mind, and would pay big money to know exactly how she was responding to this newfound knowledge. She'd seemed more than a little aroused and intrigued last night. The memory made his cock grow uncomfortably hard in his pants.

She deserves more than you've got, he reminded himself. *You'll do what you need to do to keep her safe, even if that means taking care of shit with Mikey, and even if that means spanking her ass. And then... you've gotta let her go live her own life, make her own choices.*

Donnie made himself sit back, putting some distance between himself and Grace, but her unique fragrance still filled his nostrils.

Tony brought the wine to the table, and everyone took their seats before Hillary spoke up.

"Are we missing someone?" she asked, pointing to the empty chair near the middle of the table.

"We do have one more coming," Blake said. "He'll be joining us later."

At Donnie's confused frown, Slay spoke up. "Diego. Diego

Santiago. He has some relevant information about the situation, and I wanted him to meet with us."

Down at the end of the table, Nora's head went back in surprise, but for Grace's sake, Donnie forced himself not to react outwardly to the news.

For the past few years, Diego Santiago had been undercover as a lieutenant for a cartel boss named Chalo Salazar, who'd done his best to make trouble for The Club and its members over the years. If Diego had relevant information, that meant Salazar was involved. And if Salazar was involved…. *Fuck*. The situation had just gone from bad to worse, *much worse*.

Blake cleared his throat. "So, what was Donnie teasing you about, babe?" he asked Elena, breaking the sudden anxious silence that had settled over the table. "Do I need to defend your honor?"

"Yes! He said I'm *old*," Elena accused, playing along.

Blake laughed. "Don't listen to a word he says, gorgeous. If you were any younger, they'd arrest me."

The whole table chuckled at this. The fact that Blake was twenty-five years Elena's senior had been a major factor that had kept them apart for months. Any fool could see how solid their relationship was, and how perfectly they completed each other, but their age difference had remained a running joke.

"You know, Blake, I think you may have to call Don out after all," Slay said, grabbing the platter of garlic bread that Allie handed him and putting a large slice on his plate before passing the platter to Grace.

Grace glanced from Slay to Donnie in confusion.

"Yeah?" Blake asked mildly, cutting into his chicken. "Pistols at dawn?"

"Yup. If you ask *me*, it sounded like Donnie was coming on to your woman," Slay maintained, shooting a wink in Grace's direction so she'd know he was kidding.

"By calling her *old*? You don't think my game's smoother than that?" Donnie asked, helping himself to chicken as the platter was passed in his direction.

"I'm just saying, it's an established *fact* that you have a thing for old ladies," Slay said around a mouthful of pasta. "Something about the senior citizens must really rev your engine."

The entire table burst out laughing. Matteo, in particular, laughed so loudly that he choked on his wine and Hillary had to whack him on the back.

Grace smiled, but looked at Donnie with wide, confused eyes.

Donnie sighed and aimed a sour glance at Slay. "If you're gonna bring that up, you'd better explain," he growled at the other man. "Before Grace thinks I'm a total freak."

Though he was pretty sure Grace knew enough about his kink to determine that already.

"Oh, brother, I'm happy to," Slay said, and he proceeded to regale the table with the tale of New Year's Eve a few years back, and the crush that Slay's elderly neighbor, Miss Betty, had developed on Donnie.

"She was whacking his ass, telling him to dance for her," Matteo interjected at the end, while Dom choked into his napkin and John buried his head in Paul's shoulder, practically crying with laughter. Their merriment was so loud, it woke Blake and Elena's infant daughter, Alessia, who stared around, blinking sleepily at everyone before giggling.

Donnie watched the play of emotions on Grace's face as she listened. Confusion, followed by bright laughter and then deep contentment. He could see how comfortable she'd already let herself become with this group, and it made him wish that this thing between them could be permanent somehow.

Maybe...

But before long, Tony had cleared the table of food and served up platters of creamy, flaky cannoli, and the sound of a buzzer from the rear delivery door announced Diego's arrival.

"Diego, my brother," Slay said, rising from the table to greet his friend with a handshake the moment the man walked into the room.

Diego was tall and muscular in a lean, rangy way and his golden skin was several shades darker than the last time Donnie had seen him. He strode forward with loose-limbed grace and raked his black hair off his forehead in a casual gesture that belied the way his dark eyes cased the room. Even as he returned the handshake and clapped Slay on the shoulder, Donnie was confident Diego had already mapped the location of every exit and available piece of cover, and had already calculated and ranked the most dangerous people in the room. It wasn't a conscious decision, but ingrained habit. Proper training was permanent training, after all. It was exactly what Donnie himself would do.

"You been spending time on the beach, man?" Tony joked, clearly referring to Diego's tan as he stood up to give the man his own handshake.

"Something like that," Diego agreed. "I was doing some work in Miami until two days ago." He exchanged a pointed look with Slay, who nodded as though giving his approval for Diego to speak.

Diego walked to the table and raised his hand in greeting, exchanging pleasantries with everyone. He seemed to hesitate when he glanced at Nora, who pointedly refused to look back at him, but a small, amused smirk played around his mouth as he took the empty seat.

The man seemed uncomfortable with so many people around, even knowing they were all friendly, and Donnie found himself wondering what Diego had seen and done in his years undercover... And wondering how he, himself, might have been different if he hadn't gotten out of Mikey's crew when he had.

Diego's eyes found Grace across the table. "*Hola.* You must be Miss Diaz," he said softly. His Spanish accent was pronounced, and Donnie wondered if it was natural or an affectation he'd gained undercover. Either way, he didn't like the sound of Grace's name on the man's lips.

"*Hola. Mucho gusto de conocerte,*" Grace answered politely. And though Donnie remembered enough from his high school Spanish classes to know that she'd merely said it was nice to meet Diego, something uncomfortably similar to jealousy snaked its way down Donnie's spine over this reminder that Grace and Diego shared a common language.

Without pausing to think about the statement he was making or what it revealed, Donnie slung his arm across the back of Grace's chair and leaned closer to her, so that his cheek nearly touched her soft, dark hair.

Diego's eyes met his, and the man nodded minutely, as though accepting Donnie's claim.

Then Diego smiled sadly.

"I've heard a lot about you, *mamita*," Diego told Grace softly, and the vaguely unsettled feeling in Donnie's stomach solidified into solid concrete even before Diego concluded, "Unfortunately, in the circles where I travel, that's not a good thing."

"You heard about Mikey taking her as payback?" Donnie asked, his voice a low and dangerous growl that defied anyone to argue with him. "He *thinks* he's gonna auction her off or some shit."

Diego nodded. "Least, that's how Mikey's spinning it for folks."

Baby Alessia seemed to feel the tension in the room, because she let out a long, heartbroken wail. Elena stood and walked the baby around the table to soothe her.

"That's the spin? What's the truth?" Matteo demanded, putting his arm around Hillary's shoulders.

"Well... You all know that Pedro Diaz is in the hole to Mikey, right? And Mikey's saying the debt's a cool three-quarters of a mil?" Diego asked, his eyes bouncing between Slay, Matteo, Blake, and Donnie.

Donnie nodded, and saw answering nods from the other men. But Grace gasped.

"Holy... *Holy shit*! Three-quarters of... I knew he was in debt but... Are you kidding me?" Her eyes were wild as she looked at Donnie. "How could he get that far in? Mama and I barely have enough to cover our monthly *rent*!"

"*Calmete, mamita,*" Diego said, holding up a placating hand. "Your brother stole that money from Mikey."

"And he said he paid it back," Donnie interjected.

"He did? Pedro repaid him?" Grace asked hopefully, and Diego nodded.

"He did," Diego confirmed. "But that doesn't matter anymore. The damage was already done. Mikey's demanding the same amount again as interest."

Grace closed her eyes and sighed, and Donnie pulled her closer to nestle against his chest.

"I don't get it," Allie piped up. "If the money's all been repaid..."

"Fear," Diego explained with ruthless calm. "See, men don't work for guys like Mikey or Chalo Salazar just for the money. They might start out that way, sure, if they're young and stupid. But eventually, all the money in the world isn't enough to justify the twisted shit they're asked to do." Diego's eyes were bleak. "That's where the fear comes in."

He looked up and down the table before continuing. "It's all about maintaining his reputation. Making sure everyone in the neighborhood knows how dangerous it would be to stand up to him by making an example of guys who fuck up. Sometimes a boss makes sure he has very specific evidence on his guys."

"That's what happened with Pedro," Grace admitted, folding her arms around herself. "Mikey has enough evidence to get Pedro thrown in jail for a long, long time."

Diego nodded, unsurprised. "But he's not likely to use it. The Feds would turn Pedro in a second and forgive his crimes if he testified against Mikey. No, Mikey needs to make a more personal statement… and that's where you come in," he told Grace. "Even if Pedro showed up on Mikey's doorstep tomorrow with seven hundred and fifty thousand dollars, Mikey wouldn't let you go. He's using you to prove a point to his other guys in his crew, and everyone else in the neighborhood."

"So he's *auctioning* her?" Blake demanded. "How the hell does that work?"

"The sex trade is unfortunately very much alive in Boston and everywhere else in the world," Diego said with a sigh, running both hands through his hair. "People, primarily women, but not always, are sold like property every fucking day."

"That's sick!" Nora spat, no doubt remembering how she'd been kidnapped and held by one of Chalo Salazar's guys years ago, before being rescued by Diego himself.

"It's awful," Elena agreed grimly, patting the fussy baby's back as she circled the table, and Donnie wondered whether any of the women she'd counseled at *Centered* had been victims of this type of crime.

Diego continued, shooting an apologetic glance at Grace, "But you know an auction wouldn't generate the kind of money that Mikey is claiming Pedro owes him."

Grace blinked, but it was Slay at the other end of the table who called Diego out. "It's time to spill what you know, brother."

"It's complicated." Diego's eyes met Donnie's, and burned with an intensity that said Diego had seen far more horror than he'd ever, ever discuss. "First off, Chalo Salazar has a brand new high-powered attorney, who's managed to get his parole approved. He's being released from prison next week."

A buzz ran up and down the length of the table. Chalo Salazar's name was well-known and much loathed by the people at this table. The asshole and his goons had hurt Hillary, Nora, Allie, *and* Blake over the years. Donnie watched as Matt, Tony, and Slay settled their wives closer to them, reassuring them with physical contact. Heidi rose to take the baby from Elena's arms, and Elena gave her a grateful smile before going to sit by Blake.

Diego finished, "And Mikey's planning for Grace to be his prize when he gets back to town."

Donnie pulled Grace so tightly against him that she squeaked. "Like fuck she is."

The other man nodded once, in absolute agreement. "No way, man. But like I said, the situation's complicated now. I've spent the last few months securing Chalo's interests in Miami and... *elsewhere*," Diego continued, clearly reluctant to give too much information. "And I can tell you that things are not good in

Chalo's world. The organization Chalo thought he'd return to from prison looks very different from the one he left."

"My heart breaks for him," John said bitterly, and Diego gave the man a ghost of a smile.

"Unfortunately for Chalo's men, when things aren't good, it means people get dead. And that's exactly what's been happening."

"Jesus," Tony breathed.

"Hector Montero was Salazar's top lieutenant, his second-in-command before Salazar ended up in prison. With Salazar locked up, Monterro took control of the organization. Did things his own way. No petty, vindictive bullshit for Hector, which is why The Club and all of you have been off their radar for the past couple years. The man's no angel, let me assure you. But he's no Chalo Salazar."

Donnie nodded. In the dark world where he'd grown up, there were those who were simply selfish assholes out to make money, and those, like his cousin, who seemed to take a psychotic pleasure in wielding power and torturing others. Both were criminals, but the first type was eminently preferable to the second.

Diego continued, "But Hector Montero went missing a few weeks back. We assumed it was the usual type of power grab that happens when an organization reorganizes around a major event, like Chalo's release. Lieutenants who were loyal to Chalo and the old order want to make sure that Monterro isn't going to challenge Chalo's authority once he's out. But Hector's disappearance means there's a power vacuum in the Salazar camp, and Mikey's capitalizing on that. He's stepping in and trying to prove his loyalty to Chalo. Trying to get himself an 'in' with an organization whose reach is even broader than his own."

"And how does Grace fit into this?" Donnie growled, although he was afraid he understood all too clearly

"Chalo Salazar has a documented preference for young, *innocent*, beautiful women," Diego confirmed with a sigh, shooting a brief glance at Nora. "She's Mikey Nolan's welcome home gift to Chalo. Mikey's promised to deliver her to Chalo the night after his release. If Mikey doesn't come through… well. Let's just say breaking promises is never a good way to start out a relationship."

Diego shrugged and Donnie got the feeling that there was more to the story than the other man would share at this point. He felt frustration boil beneath his skin, and could think of no good outlet. He wanted to lock Grace in his apartment, and simultaneously send her as far away from Chalo and Mikey as possible. Although if Diego's assessment of the situation was fair, Mikey was about to have a far longer reach than Slay's contacts did, and Donnie had *no* way of assuring Grace's safety, even if she agreed to let him send her away.

Fuck.

Donnie clenched his hands into fists. This situation was so far out of his control, it wasn't funny. He'd believed the solution would involve neutralizing Mikey, and although he hadn't fully admitted to himself just how far he'd go, Donnie had been ready to wade in and make that happen, by whatever means necessary. But now it seemed that fucking *Chalo Salazar* was also trying to make a claim on his Grace. No fucking *way*.

Silence fell around the table once again, and Grace lifted one shaking hand to rub her eyes. Donnie pulled her closer and pressed a gentle kiss to the side of her head. The bullshit about what kind of man she deserved and the type of life Donnie could provide her seemed pretty fucking distant and stupid in the face of this threat.

"You assumed." Nora's voice broke the quiet, and made Diego's eyes flash in her direction.

"*Perdón?*" Diego asked, his forehead wrinkled.

"You said… You said you *assumed* that's why Hector Montero went missing a few weeks back," Nora clarified, her brown eyes locked onto Diego's defiantly. "But what *really* happened?"

Diego stared at her for a moment as though he'd never seen her before, and his mouth hung open slightly, before he closed it with a snap, blanking his expression and giving her a casual shrug. "Who knows?"

But his hesitation had been obvious and confirmed Donnie's earlier suspicion.

"If there's more information that we need to know…" Donnie began, flattening his hand on the table.

Diego hesitated, pursing his lips and glancing at Slay, who simply nodded. Then Diego said, "Slay trusts everyone at this table, so I'm gonna trust you too. But I need you to understand that the information I'm about to give you is not just sensitive, it's extremely dangerous. Dangerous for *me* to give you, and dangerous for *you* to have… but it might also keep you safe."

Up and down the table, heads nodded uneasily.

"We've known for quite some time that Salazar's not working independently. He simply doesn't have the manpower or the money to do the shit he does without a backer. Several years ago, after we attempted to take him down on drug charges," he said, glancing at Allie, who'd been injured as an indirect result of that attempted bust, "we discovered Salazar was affiliated with a larger crime syndicate in Mexico that primarily ran drugs along the East Coast. But once Salazar became front page news, that cartel backed off. Left Salazar twisting in the wind for a bit. Now, though... he's found himself a new sponsor."

"Who?" Nora demanded.

Diego met her eyes squarely. "We just don't know." He glanced around the table. "All communications from prison are monitored, and it's unclear how this sponsorship started. All we know is that Chalo refers to this person as *El Jefe*, the boss. And El Jefe doesn't deal in drugs, he deals in flesh. The sex trade, like we discussed before."

"*Christ*," Blake said, leaning back in his chair. The glance he shot at Diego was pitying, and once again Donnie wondered what shit Diego had been forced to see and do in order to maintain his cover.

Donnie hugged Grace tighter.

When Diego spoke again, he sounded tired. "Yet another reason why Mikey wants to publicize this thing with Grace, and spread the rumor that it's an auction. He wants an in with Salazar, yes, but if that doesn't work, he'll know he's built cred with *El Jefe*."

"So worst case scenario, he can cut Salazar out completely and take a stab at working directly for the big fish," Nora concluded, eyes narrowed in thought.

Once again, Diego stared at her in puzzled fascination before nodding. "*Si, exactamente.* The way your brain works, Norita..."

Tony snorted. "No shit. Sometimes she frightens the crap out of me."

"Hey!" Nora argued, her cheeks pinkening as she glared at her brother-in-law.

Donnie waved a hand impatiently, cutting off Nora's outrage. "So in the meantime, what the fuck do we do? How do we keep Grace safe?"

Diego sighed. "We need time. We're working every avenue we can think of to find *El Jefe's* identity. We're calling in favors across the board, working our informants."

"What about a forensic accountant?" Heidi asked, as she passed behind Donnie, still walking Elena and Blake's restless daughter. "Trace the source of any payments to Salazar, and you can find out *El Jefe's* identity."

Diego shook his head. "We don't know that any money has exchanged hands. Salazar's in prison, and it's too early in the partnership."

Heidi shook her head. "Nonsense. Didn't you say Salazar had some new high-powered attorney?"

Diego blinked. "I… yeah. He does."

"Where'd he get the money for a new attorney?" Paul wondered aloud.

Donnie remembered that Heidi and Paul ran some kind of financial analysis company, and that's how Dom and Heidi had met.

Diego looked taken aback, as though this were an avenue that he hadn't considered, and Donnie's heart sped up.

"Fuck. Okay, yeah," Diego said excitedly. "Let me make some calls."

"I'm happy to help if you need me," Paul told him.

Diego nodded distractedly before pushing himself to his feet. He shook his head as if to collect himself, then spoke. "In the meantime, Pedro is as safe as we can make him, and we're moving Mrs. Diaz to a safe location, as well. Grace should stay with you guys, but be aware. Once Salazar is released from prison and they know Grace is missing, things are going to get dangerous very quickly."

"Grace and I can go to—" Donnie began, but Slay cut him off.

"Bad idea, Don. You heard Diego. They need *time*. I get that your instincts tell you to jump on your bike and take your girl far away," he said, reading Donnie's mind. "But we have no idea whether activity outside The Clubs is being monitored in preparation for Salazar's release. They'd notice a huge change in routine like you taking off, and that'd be a major red flag that could tip Mikey off way before we're ready."

"Agreed," Blake said. "I think Grace should continue to stay with you at The Club right now. You've got tight security in place, and we can put Grace into lockdown once Salazar is released. No one needs to know she's there."

Diego nodded, then walked around the edge of the table and paused next to Grace's chair. "I promise you, Miss Diaz, we'll do everything we can to keep you safe, and to get you your life back," he told her.

Grace simply nodded, her cheek rubbing against Donnie's shirt as she leaned against him, and Donnie could tell she'd reached the end of what she could handle right then. He was suddenly eager to get her out of here, take her home, tuck her in bed, and watch over her all night.

Diego looked at Donnie, a question in his eyes, and Donnie gave him a nod, as well. If Slay, Matteo, and Blake trusted the man, Donnie would too.

But he wouldn't let down his guard or relax one iota until he was sure Grace was safe.

Chapter 6

Grace rubbed her hand across her eyes, fingers gently wiping away the haze of sleep and dreams. Had she been dreaming? As her eyes adjusted to the dim morning light, and her subconscious turned to waking, she realized she wasn't alone. However, the large, shadowy figure sitting on the edge of the bed was welcome.

"Morning, sunshine." Donnie's gravelly voice came low in the dimness of early morning, and she could hear the smile in his voice. He was wearing only light blue boxers and a thin white t-shirt, a sight Grace could get used to. He handed her a mug of steaming hot coffee. "Rise and shine."

She closed her eyes, burrowed deeper under the covers belly down, and grunted. Nope, Not getting up yet. The night before, Donnie had checked on The Club before bed, and paused to check his email. When he'd sent her upstairs, some girl—Grace recognized her as the girl whose ass had been on display while Donnie did his demonstration—had intercepted her on the stairs. She'd been sweet, and asked if Grace had needed anything. So sweet, in fact, that Grace convinced herself she'd likely imagined the look of fury she'd seen on the woman's face the night of the session. Grace had been tired, though and excused herself, instead choosing to peruse the iPad for something to do while she waited for Donnie to come upstairs.

Having met Hillary, she'd been more curious to read her books. She'd loved his friends, and felt as if she'd known them far longer than the one night, and Hillary felt like a friend already. She'd chosen one of Hillary's books, and had been up half the night reading. She was now in no mood to get up. "Hmmmph," she said to him.

His voice lowered warningly. "Gracie."

"Mmmph."

The clink of the coffee mug indicated he'd put it down on the bedside table, and the next thing she knew, the bedcovers were being yanked off unceremoniously, the cool air grazing her bare legs. Her eyes flew open and she gasped, but it was too late. His wide, broad palm slapped her thinly-clad bottom, not once but three times, hard swats that woke her up more effectively than the call of a boot camp bugle.

"Ow! Give me those blankets!" She sat up, reaching for the covers, but he held them out of her reach, his eyes both dancing and heated.

"Keep acting the part of the brat, and I'll wake you up over my knee," he said.

She flopped back on the pillows and sighed dramatically. "Okay, Donnie. You win." Now she wanted the blankets not just because her legs were cold, but because the few sharp spanks and threat of more had made her panties dampen and her nipples tighten against the thin t-shirt she'd worn to bed. His eyes traveled down past hers, to her breasts, and lingered. She watched as he swallowed.

"You always sleep in just a t-shirt?" he asked, tossing her the blanket and tearing his gaze away.

She couldn't help but tease him. "No, usually I sleep in the nude but I've made myself have at least a scrap of decorum, seeing as it's your bed."

"Fuck," he groaned. "You really are a brat."

Grace stifled a giggle, sitting up in bed and reaching for the coffee cup. "Ask an honest question, get an honest answer," she retorted. The coffee was steaming hot, creamy and sweet, just like she liked it. She moaned. "Oh, this is good stuff," she said.

He grinned, sending a shock wave of arousal straight between her legs. It wasn't fair how he could do that. She swallowed another scalding sip of coffee, just so she could get her shit together.

"So why the early morning wake-up call?" she said, still feeling the sting of his palm on her skin as she sipped her coffee. It was not unpleasant, sitting here in his bed, wearing nothing but a t-shirt and a pair of panties, with the reminder of his dominance throbbing against the sheets.

He inhaled, and sat up straighter. "Gotta get shit done today," he said. "And there's no real reason I woke you up," he said, suddenly looking a little sheepish. He shrugged. "I just wanted to see you before I left, and you were sleeping later than you ever do, so I thought it was time I helped you along."

She smiled into the coffee mug. He'd wanted to see her?

"What day is today?" she asked, suddenly realizing that while she'd been away, the days and times had bled together, and she no longer had a firm grasp on when it was.

"Thursday," he said, standing and stretching, as he walked over to the window and opened the shade. She reached for the iPad she'd left next to her, and flicked it on. Thursday, *May 2nd.*

Oh my God. How had she lost track of the time so much that she hadn't realized it was her birthday? She stared at the date, overcome with a myriad of emotions. If she were at home, her mama would've baked her a cake, and had her presents wrapped and waiting for her on the breakfast table, just like she always had. Grace would've taken the day off from work, and done something fun, just for herself, maybe wandered into one of those used bookstores in town, the ones with the fragrant smell of time-worn paper and leather bindings, then bought herself a steaming latte and treated herself to something new.

But not today. No, today, she was stuck in a third-floor apartment with the man of her dreams, who'd just seen her in nothing but a pair of panties and he hadn't even kissed her.

How had she ever thought she'd be good enough for him?

She slammed the iPad down on the bedside table, unaware of the fact he'd spoken until she realized he'd stopped.

"What's that all about?" he asked, his brows furrowed as he still stood in front of the windows. "Why are you pissed all of a sudden?"

She shook her head. "It's nothing," she lied, glad she had the excuse of a cup of coffee to nurse so she could continue brooding in silence.

Donnie's lips thinned and a muscle ticked in his jaw. "Nothing?" he asked, his tone implying that he well knew she was lying.

Don't lie to me, Grace.

Though her heart thumped, she nodded silently. He finally released her from his glare, as he walked to the door, muttering something about women being a complete mystery to him. "I have to get going," he said. "There's food in the kitchen, and more coffee if you need it. I'll come back at lunchtime to check on you, and if I call you on the cell, you *answer*. Got it?"

She nodded. "Yeah."

He turned to fix her with another stern glare, which made her squirm. What was that all about?

But he merely shook his head and left.

Grace resisted the temptation to whip her coffee mug across the room, and suddenly realized she *was* acting like a total brat. This was not who she was. What had gotten into her?

A while later, she heard the door click, indicating he'd gone downstairs to work. Sighing, she got up out of bed. Because he'd already left, she didn't bother putting her pants on. Her stomach growled with hunger, as she hadn't eaten much the night before.

Padding to the kitchen, she screamed out loud when she ran smack dab into Donnie.

"Whoa, girl!" he said, his hands coming to rest on her shoulders and hold her apart from him. "Why are you screaming like you just saw a ghost? You didn't know I was here?"

"I heard the door shut!" she protested. "I thought you were gone!"

"I was just putting out the recycling," he said. "I haven't left yet."

"Clearly," she muttered.

He pulled her closer to him, his hand smoothing over her panties. He squeezed her ass hard enough to make her squeal. "That why you didn't bother putting clothes on?" he asked. "You thought I wasn't here?"

She swallowed, her cheek pressed up against his t-shirt. "Yes," she whispered.

"Putting clothes on would be a good idea," he said in her ear, as his hand traveled from her ass up to her lower back, and he pulled her even closer to him, so close she could feel his erection pressed up against her. God, he was turned on. Her stoic bodyguard was *turned on*.

"Okay," she breathed. He released her and she nearly stumbled as he walked away.

"Now I'm going, honey," he said. "Go eat breakfast and get dressed, and I'll be back in an hour or so. Yeah?"

She nodded. "Okay," she whispered, watching him go, wondering where exactly she stood with him and how she would ever figure it out.

A short while later, she'd showered and dressed, and was sitting in the living room, reading the book she'd started the night before, determined to distract herself from everything. Whatever. It was just a day, and that guy Diego had made it clear that her mama was safe. That was the most important thing.

Safe.

Grace sighed, grateful for the book she was reading. She needed the distraction to keep her mind off of Donnie, and her mama, safe houses, and drug lords. *God*. If she didn't occupy her mind, she'd start right down that road again where she managed to convince herself she was nothing to Donnie. Anyway, things had just started heating up in her book.

The door creaked open, then slammed shut. She jumped. Why was he back so soon? She heard him stalking through the front room, then he was standing in the doorway, looking absolutely pissed off. His hands were on his hips, his eyes blazing.

"Gracia Maria Diaz," he said.

Oh. Oh, *hell*. He was pissed all right. She couldn't ever recall him calling her by her full name. And *damn*, why was he so *hot* when he was pissed?

"Um. Yes?" she said, her heart tripping in her chest, and her panties dampening. *God.*

"Why didn't you fucking *tell* me it was May *second?* You thought you'd keep it all to yourself? You thought somehow I would *forget?*" He was stalking over to her now, his heavy boots clomping on the hardwood floor as he marched his way over to her. She pushed her back up against the loveseat, but it was a fruitless endeavor, as he was a mere foot away now, and when he reached her—

"Ahhhh! Donnie! Put me *down!*" she said, flailing her arms as she found herself soaring up out of the loveseat and dumped over his lap.

No *way.* Was he going to spank her for not telling him it was her birthday?

Her heart stuttered, her hands grasping the edge of the love seat as she felt him lower her pants. Holy shit!

Oh my God.

"Donnn*iiiieeee*," she wailed. "What are you doing?"

It was obvious what he was doing. What else would he be doing? She'd been over his knee twice now, and she knew that when he dumped her over his lap belly-down, it was because she was about to get her ass spanked, but she couldn't help but protest.

"I didn't do anything wrong!" she said. "You told me if I put myself in danger you'd sp—oww!"

His hand had come down and slapped against her panties. *Yeowch that hurt.*

"Count 'em," he growled.

"One!" she shouted out loud. "Donnie, what the hell! Ow!"

Whack.

"Count!"

"Two!"

"Very good. I seem to recall you're six years younger than me. So that makes you twenty-six. You get twenty-six birthday spanks."

Holy shit!

He punctuated his statement with another slap of his palm. She counted her way to seven in a blur of confusion and arousal, not fully grasping what was happening until he reached ten, and by then, her pulse had accelerated, and she could feel the dampness of her panties as she squirmed over his lap. It seemed he could, too, for at this point, he spread her legs with his broad, warm palm, and one finger dragged along the thin strip of fabric covering her sex.

Oh *God*. The smell of sex, arousal, and longing permeated her senses.

"We were at ten," he growled. "And now I think you're warmed up."

His fingers were on the edge of her panties now, pulling them down slowly, like he was unwrapping a present.

"Donnie!" she gasped. He'd see she was wet. "Oh, no. Please don't! I…"

Another hard spank, this time on her naked skin, left her howling.

"Count," he ordered.

"Eleven!" She counted out four more spanks, and by now, she didn't care that he knew she was aroused. All that she wanted was his hands on her.

At fifteen, she wriggled her pussy up against his lap, looking for something, some kind of pressure or release, but he was still spanking her. Every thwack of his hand on her naked skin sent shock waves of delight zinging to her clit. God, she was so turned on.

At twenty, she was holding onto her self control by a mere thread, and silently begging for release, writhing on his knee, the heated sting on her skin only making her arousal flare uncontrollably.

"Twenty-two," she panted, two swats later. He paused, rubbing his rough hand over her hot skin before lifting his palm and bringing it down again with another stinging smack. "Twenty-three!" she shrieked. With his left hand, he wrapped her hair around his hand and pulled, before delivering another swat. "Twenty-four," she moaned. Another rapid spank followed another, and she exhaled. Finally, they were done.

"And one for good luck," he growled, giving her the hardest spank he'd given her yet.

"Ow!"

He was done now. Her cheeks were flaming hot, but her body was on fire. What would he do to her next? Slowly, his hand lifted and he replaced her panties as she raised herself up, pushing off the loveseat, but when the time came for her to look at him, she lost her resolve and buried her face on his chest.

"You gonna be a good birthday girl?" he said, a thread of humor in his voice now.

"You're not mad?" she said, smiling into his shirt.

"Nah, babe. I was pissed at first."

"That I didn't tell you it was my birthday?" she giggled, the absurdity of the situation suddenly striking her, while she became blissfully aware of the scent of him, leather and musk, as she sat engulfed in his arms.

"Yup," he said. "You knew, and that's why you got all pissy this morning, and you didn't tell me."

"Didn't know I was supposed to," she said, with another laugh. *Or that you cared,* she thought.

He pushed her gently off his chest and one large, rough finger tipped her chin up, so she was looking straight into his dark brown eyes, his square jaw framed with sandy-colored stubble, his hair hitting his chin.

"Why wouldn't I want to know?" he said.

Ignoring the obvious response, she answered his question with a question. "How did you find out?" she asked, still aware of his finger under her chin.

"Got downstairs. Paid some bills. Saw the date," he said, his eyes darkening. "I know your birthday, honey. I just didn't remember today was it."

Ohh. Well, huh.

She looked away, but his hand tightened on her chin, bringing her eyes back to his. "I've called in backup today, so we have the day off."

She blinked, and swallowed, then blinked again. "You did?" she whispered, not trusting her voice.

"Yep. Gonna celebrate your birthday right," he said. His eyes traveled downward, and she realized she was sitting her freshly-spanked, panty-clad bottom on his lap. She could feel his hard-on straight through the thin fabric.

"How does one celebrate a birthday right?" she whispered, as his head dipped closer to hers.

"You start with a birthday spanking," he said. "Then you get a cake. And you get something good to drink. And you do something just for you."

"Just for you?" she asked. "Like what?" Her breath was a

mere whisper as his fingers spread over her jaw, cupping her face and gently tipping her face up toward his. "Like... like with a kiss?" *From the man of your dreams? The one you'd give anything to be with?*

His lips tipped up a second before he kissed her, soft and sweet. Her ass throbbed and her body arched closer to him, wanting more than the chaste kiss. His left hand went to the small of her back, the warm touch making her feel precious to him, as his right hand gently entwined around a fistful of her hair. He pulled away, groaning, tossing his head back on the couch.

"Jesus," he muttered.

"What?" she felt sudden disappointment hit, yet hope fluttered at his obvious arousal.

"I lose all control when I'm around you," he said. "Been trying years to get myself under control and all you have to do is bat those eyelashes and I come undone."

Grace tucked her head shyly, hiding the grin that she couldn't control, not sure just exactly how much to push her luck. She shrugged. "Not sure I mind," she said.

She felt his hands on her shoulders as he shook her, his eyes suddenly sobering. "Hey," he said. "You *should* mind. It's not right for any old guy to just take advantage of you."

His tone rose her ire, and her head snapped back up. "I *don't* let just any old guy take advantage of me," she said. "How do you think I got to twenty-six still a virgin? For real? You think you're just any old guy?"

God, no. She wanted to slap him straight across his beautiful face, but knew she'd pay the price.

His jaw clenched. "I'm not what you need, Grace. You don't need some guy who gets off on dishing out pain. You don't need a guy who likes control. You need some guy with a fucking B.A. who will make your mama proud. A guy with a real car, not the back of my bike."

Her stomach clenched and her nose stung. Still sitting on his lap suddenly felt comical. She yanked at her pants as she pushed off his lap, pulling them up as she stood, marching toward the door.

"Oh yeah?" she said over her shoulder. "Fuck this, Donnie. How nice of you to give me *control* over everything by deciding exactly what it is that I do and do not *want* or need." She blindly walked, not thinking about where she'd go or what she'd do, but knowing she couldn't stay another minute in this stifling apartment.

"Grace—"

"No! I've lived my whole life with other people telling me what to do, and I'm *sick* of it!" she shouted, only paces away from the door now. She heard him get to his feet, as her hand reached for the doorknob.

"Grace, *stop.*"

She froze, her hand on the doorknob, as she whipped around to face him.

"What? So you can tell me what else I need? A white picket fence in suburbia with the swing set and tricycles? Seriously, Donnie? Do you have any idea what *I* want? Has it ever occurred to you to ask *me?*"

His eyes flashed, arms crossed on his chest, but she saw a flicker of pain cross his face, and she knew she'd somehow hit home.

"Get your hand off the doorknob." The words were spoken in a low, calm tone, but she knew it was the tone that meant he expected her to do what she was told. Her ass still throbbing, she released the door knob and clenched her jaw, folding her own arms petulantly over her chest for emphasis.

Fine, I'll obey but you won't make me do it nicely.

As he raised a brow, her pulse quickened, and she dropped both her arms and her gaze.

It appeared he would.

"Come here."

She wanted to. Oh, how she wanted to. But what if the stand-off was because she wasn't good enough for him? She didn't have the figure of that girl downstairs. She didn't know a damn thing about doms or subs or what they *did* in a place like this, though the friends of his she'd met were... normal enough.

She looked at him across the room, and when she spoke, her voice wobbled. "What if I don't want to?" she whispered.

"Gracie," he said, his voice growing soft, as his arms opened up to her. "Honey, you do. You know you do. Now c'mere." He sobered, his voice deepening. "And you know if you step one foot out that door, I'll give you the spanking of your little life."

Her pulse spiked as she walked to him on trembling legs. Where would she go? Who else would take care of her? In seconds, she was back in his arms, burying her face on his chest as he held her close. Why had she been angry? Was she going crazy?

"Tell me, Gracie," he said, his hand on the back of her neck, possessive and soothing, as he held her face up to his chest. "Tell me what *you* want. Not what anyone else wants for you, not even me. What do *you* want?"

"What do I want?" she whispered.

"Yeah, babe. What does Grace Diaz *want?*"

"I don't want a house in suburbia and a guy in a suit, Donnie. I want a man who knows me, the *real* me, so well, he'd do anything to protect me, even if that means... putting me on the back of his bike, and taking me to his very own place, where he can keep an eye on me, so I don't get hurt. I want a man who loves fiercely, who's strong and steady. I want someone to watch over me." Her voice shook strangely, and she closed her eyes. "I want *you.*"

He sighed, holding her close to him.

"Donnie, I don't know what tomorrow will bring. I know that I lost you once, and I don't want to lose you again. I don't know if tomorrow I'll still be here, or if Chalo-whatever will find me, or if-if... Mikey will track me down, or if they'll come and get me."

"Baby," he said, pulling her to him fiercely. "They're *not* gonna get you. I'll kill them before they get you." She heard it then, the street boy she'd grown up with who broke legs and jaws without apology, her hero, the one who'd protect her when no one else could. He would; he'd kill every last one standing up for her.

"I know," she whispered. "God, Donnie." The moment could be lost, and the brilliant clarity she had then could flit away. She had to say it. "What if today is the last day we have?"

"Grace," he said, his voice pained. "No, baby. Stop."

But she would not be deterred. She lifted her head and looked into his eyes, both of her hands on his shoulders now. "No, Donnie," she said, shaking her head. "You asked me, and I'm only answering. What if I die a twenty-six-year-old virgin? And I never told the one man I'd pledged my life to that I loved him? I love you. And I don't want to lose you."

Her voice shook, tears on her cheeks now, but she did nothing to stop them.

He shook his head, his eyes on hers probing. "God, Grace. You're not gonna lose me, honey. You're not—"

"Then make me *yours*, Donnie. Damn it!" Her voice rose in desperation. "I'm not that little girl anymore. I'm a woman. You asked me what I wanted, and I told you. I want *you. You.*" She was crying freely now as he lifted her up in his arms, her legs encircling his waist, while he walked her to his bedroom. She leaned in to kiss him, needing to taste him, needing him to *know* how serious she was with more than her words.

Lowering her onto the pillows as he knelt down next to her, he lifted his mouth off hers just long enough to whisper a heated, tortured, "*Grace.*"

"Make me yours, Donnie," she begged. "*Please.*" And she didn't know how or why, but she was filled with certainty, a clarity that everything had led to this moment. "Let my first time making love be with a man who cares about me, Donnie. Let it be with someone who knows me, and who wants to make my first time special." Her voice cracked, as he leaned in and kissed her cheek, her whole world consumed by him, his scent and warmth, the beating of his heart, and the way he held her close, as if somehow he couldn't get her close enough.

Releasing her just long enough to snag the end of his shirt and pull it off, she sighed in contentment, running her hands over his strong, muscled chest, needing to feel his naked skin against her palm. He lowered himself down to her, kissing her softly again, his hands at her top now, lifting it up. As he bared her, her breasts nearly spilling out of the top of her bra, he groaned out loud. With a tortured moan, he pulled her pants down. She lifted her hips as the fabric slid slowly down over her bare legs, beckoning him, begging him to take her.

She was laying on *Donnie's bed*, stripped to nothing but her panties and bra, and he was kneeling over her, her big, strong, muscled, *hero* was staring down at her with nothing short of adoration.

Her fantasy had come to life.

"Gonna make you mine, angel."

Her sob caught in her throat as his mouth came to hers, sweet and gentle, like only a man with the strength of a giant could be, as if she were spun glass in need of a tender touch. His mouth went to her neck, his warm, whiskery kiss making her thighs clench together in a sweeping wave of arousal. His tongue flicked out in a sensual gesture that set tingles down her spine, as his hands went to her waist.

"I want you to have *special*, Grace," he whispered in her ear. "I need you good and ready for me."

"God, I'm ready," she groaned, and he only shook his head, as he removed her bra. Lowering his mouth to the valley between her breasts, his warm, soft tongue tracing a path to the pink peak of her nipple. He took one breast in his mouth while his hand traveled between her legs, the tips of his fingers dragging down the edge of her panties. One finger dipped low, stroking her slowly, as his mouth did wonderful, torturous things to her breast.

"Nice and ready," he whispered. "I don't want to hurt you."

Hurt her? The only thing that would hurt her now would be if he stopped.

He lifted his mouth from her breast and whispered in her ear. "I like things rough, angel. I like inflicting pain. I call the shots in here. But today, this is about you, and today you need gentle."

She shivered in delight. She knew he could be rough. Her ass bore witness to the sting of his palm, and she well knew she'd only had a taste of what he had to offer. But knowing he *could* be rough made his gentle ministrations just that much sweeter.

He released her just long enough to slide his own jeans down, the length of his erection tenting his boxers as he knelt back down to her. His hands cupped her breasts, his thumbs flicking over her sensitive nipples once more until she thought she could climax from that touch alone.

"Donnie," she panted, her head falling to the side, hips bucking. "Oh, God."

"Not yet, Gracie."

He pried her legs apart with one knee, and she gratefully opened for him, as he lowered himself down. Slowly, his hands dragged the length of her body, her panties grazing over her curves as he moved them down and lowered his mouth.

"Ohhhh, no," she said, suddenly embarrassed at the thought of whatever he planned to do.

Slow, delicious, lazy laps of his tongue along her slit made her moan. "Donnie," she gasped.

"Need you ready," he said, lifting his mouth off of her just long enough to whisper, before he returned to the delicious assault of her senses.

"I'm going to…" she began, and he was up, pushing his boxers down, holding his massive body over hers as he gently spread her legs even wider.

"You'll wait, Gracie. That's it. Open wide and relax. Do you trust me, angel?"

"So much," she said, her voice shaking. "I trust you with everything." This was it, the moment when he'd make her his, and when he did, there would be no going back. Her *hero* would make her his, and things would never be the same again.

Bracing himself over her, he gently probed, his own breath suspended as if time were paused. "I don't want to hurt you," he whispered.

"I trust you," she said.

"Need protection, baby," he said. He reached for his bedside table, removing a condom and sliding it along his erection as his eyes bore into hers. Her heart beat in thunderous anticipation, on the cusp of something so monumental she could hardly breathe. Slowly, carefully, and so gently, he entered her, and she could feel the way he was holding back, his leashed strength as he filled her. There was the barest twinge of pain as he stretched her, but it faded as he slowly built a rhythm, and with each slow, firm thrust of his hips, electric waves of pleasure shot through her. "Does it hurt, Grace?" he whispered, holding her tight against him.

"It's perfect," she answered, because it was. Nothing could've prepared her for what it felt like to be connected to him like this, the combination of pleasure-pain bringing her closer to ecstasy as she lay beneath him, surrendered to him in the most vulnerable of ways. The tempo of his thrusts increased. He was panting now, and she felt herself building. Everything he did was a delicious contradiction—slow and fast, pain and pleasure, full but not enough. "Don't stop," she breathed. "God, Donnie, this is so good. So, so good. Please, honey."

His breath was ragged with every move of his hips, and he held his body weight off of hers so that she felt both warmed and secure beneath him. "That's it, angel," he said. "God, you feel so perfect, Grace." He closed his eyes. "So perfect."

"I can't—" she gasped. "I'm going to—"

She couldn't hold on another second and his words only made her want to let it all go, where she was safe and free and treasured. "Come for me. Gracie, baby. I love you. Come, honey."

She climaxed with abandon, her hips jerking upward as he

groaned, her head falling back against the pillow, as her hands grasped onto his strong, muscled arms. He held her tight, her body pressed up against his as the two of them came as one. She rode the waves of pleasure until they both lay spent, and as she settled into the warmth of his arms, she did nothing to staunch the flow of tears that freely fell.

"Grace," he said, looking at her with concern. "Did I hurt you? God, if I hurt you—"

"No," she sniffled, shaking her head. "I'm crying because that was so right. You... me... us... like this." And her tears flowed harder.

His eyes softened, his lips quirking as he brought his mouth to her forehead in a tender kiss that warmed her through.

"I love you, Grace Diaz," he whispered in her ear. "I always have, and I always will."

Chapter 7

I love you, Grace Diaz.

The moment the words left his mouth, he'd almost wished he could call them back, not because they were untrue, they fucking *weren't*, but because of the way Grace's face changed when he spoke them. She leaned up on one elbow and stared at him, her big, brown eyes liquid in the morning light, as if he were some Prince Charming or a fantasy come to life. Nothing could be further from the truth.

Fuck, he wished he were worthy of that look.

But it was too late to grab the words back, just like it was too late to undo what they'd done.

He'd taken her virginity.

Something fierce and primal rose up in him as he acknowledged that even if it *could* be undone, he *wouldn't*. He'd known exactly what he was doing when he took her, claimed her, marked her as his. She belonged to him now; not to Mikey, or Chalo, or any other "better" man, and she was stuck with him forever. God help her.

In the heat of the moment, he'd told her no less than the

truth. There was a dark part of him that pulsed with the need to inflict pain on a willing partner, that took satisfaction from knowing that they *enjoyed* the pain, too. But hurting *Grace* was a concept that was entirely foreign to him. And he resolved then and there that no part of his darkness would ever touch her. For her, he'd push that desire down into nothingness.

She clearly enjoyed the spanking and the discipline that he provided her, and even *that* was a thousand times more than he ever would have hoped for with her... If he'd ever allowed himself to really imagine a life with Grace in the first place. So that would be enough.

"Donnie?" she asked, still watching him with those big eyes, but hesitant now as though his silence had made her uneasy.

He smiled broadly and cupped her cheek with one large hand, brushing aside the moisture that remained there.

"You ready for part two?" he asked with a wink.

Her eyes widened and she bit her lip, before glancing down his body. "Really? Can we do it again already?"

Donnie threw back his head and laughed. *Oh, FUCK, but he loved her.*

"Eh... not quite yet, angel," he told her, feeling his cock twitch in a way that let him know his body was definitely interested in following her line of thought. "Better to wait. You might be a little sore."

She moved, flexing her muscles experimentally, and frowned at him. "I think you read too many romance novels, honey. I feel *fine.*"

"Is that so?" he asked, threading his fingers through her hair and pulling her face to his.

She broke into a wide grin and nodded, making their lips

bump. "In fact, I'm thinking maybe I need to make up for lost time."

He gave into temptation and took her mouth more fully with his, cradling her jaw in his palm as their tongues tangled, but just as her cool hands began to roam across the hard planes of his chest and her breathing ramped up, he eased her back.

"We will definitely get back to *this* later. But you've got a birthday to celebrate, so up you go. *Now*, Miss Diaz," he told her when she pouted.

"Or maybe *this* could be my birthday celebration?" she asked, fluttering her eyelashes hopefully. Her eyelids were at half-mast, her eyes cloudy with arousal, and her lips were swollen and rosy from their kisses. He bit back a groan, and instead reached down to smack her bottom with his other hand.

"Donnie!" she complained, jumping slightly. "*That* part of me *is* sore, and I don't see you showing *it* any consideration."

Donnie snorted before leaning over to steal one last quick kiss and then moving her gently away from him. "Nope. When it comes to that fine ass of yours, Gracie, you'll find that I'm a big fan of natural consequences."

"Natural consequences," she repeated, leaning her head down on her folded arms and watching him as he grabbed his clothes and began to tug his boxers and jeans back on.

"Yep. The more disobedient you are, the more your ass will throb." He held out his hands like weighing scales. "Better that you learn this lesson sooner than later, baby. If you don't like the pain, don't disobey."

She watched him closely for a moment, her gaze serious and unmoving. "And what if I do like the pain?" she asked softly.

His breath hitched.

The woman had no idea what she was asking, of course. And

no idea that her simple words were making the blood pound in his veins.

"Spanking can be fun, angel. But it can also be serious. You don't want to disobey me, now, do you?"

She squirmed, and he remembered the way she'd cried when he'd spanked her for real. No. No, she didn't like letting him down, and she'd learn to do as she was told.

He forced himself to stand up, buttoning his jeans as he calmly turned the conversation. "I remember what you like, and it could usually be found at the *Panaderia Marquez*."

She blinked. "At the… you mean the little Puerto Rican bakery over in The Heights? But that closed down years ago."

Donnie nodded. "But I found a little shop just like it not two miles from here. Perfect place to get your favorite birthday cake."

"*Tres leches?*" she breathed, her eyes wide.

He couldn't help the grin that rose to his face. God, his girl was sweet, nearly as sweet as the whipped-cream-topped cake she loved. "Yup," he confirmed. "Get cleaned up while I take care of a couple things in the office. I'll come back for you in a bit and we can go."

She pushed herself up to a seated position, tucking the sheet under her arms to cover herself, and Donnie grinned. As fiery as his girl was, he didn't foresee that modesty lasting too long, so he'd let it stand… for now.

He tugged his shirt into place.

"And don't forget what comes after that," she teased. "Something good to drink?" He rolled his eyes. "And then something just for me."

"Hmmm." He took a step toward the bed and leaned over her, so his face was inches from hers. "I thought we determined that you already got what you wanted," he argued.

Her smile was blinding. "But it wasn't really *just for me*, was it?"

He shook his head. Man, he was a sucker for this woman. He opened his mouth to retort, eager to see how she would respond and the light that would flash in her eyes, but before the words would come, the blaring sound of a fire alarm assaulted his ears.

Shit. Not again.

"Let's go, princess," he yelled above the screeching, grabbing her clothes from the floor and dropping her shirt over her head.

"Donnie! I need my bra!" she protested as he tore back the sheet and glided her panties up her legs. He almost snickered. Seemed he'd be challenging her modesty even sooner than he'd anticipated.

"No time," he told her, knowing that his amusement was likely visible on his face when she narrowed her eyes. "I'm almost sure it's a false alarm. Stupid system's been glitchy for a coupla weeks. But we're not taking any chances."

"But I…"

He wrapped his hands around her waist and lifted her bodily off the bed before placing her on the floor so she was flush against him.

"Did I somehow indicate that I wanted you to argue with me?" he demanded, his mouth against her ear.

"No, but—"

"And you do remember what happens when you disobey my orders and put your safety at risk, yeah?" He kept his tone even, but it was clear that he was one hundred percent serious.

She was silent as he took a step back. She grabbed her pants off the bed and stepped into them, but the way her eyes locked on his and her cheeks flushed with irritation told him that she was *not* pleased.

He felt his cock harden and his palms sting with the need to melt her anger. Instead, he bent over to grab her shoes, then he pulled her out the door and down the stairs.

As they passed the second floor, Connie and the head bartender, Andy, walked out of the office, their heads still bent together over a clipboard Connie held. Likely, they were reviewing the order form for the following week. But as they reached the stairs, they looked up and saw Donnie, and then followed his outstretched arm to where Grace trailed behind. Both of them stopped short.

Donnie swore under his breath.

Through sheer luck, he'd managed to keep Grace's presence in the building from becoming general knowledge among the staff. No one seemed to have noticed her presence the night that she'd snuck downstairs and watched his demonstration, and she hadn't been downstairs otherwise unless The Club was deserted.

It hadn't occurred to him that he and Grace would attract much notice as they exited the building, either. But maybe it was too much to expect his employees not to notice that their boss was holding hands with someone who had very clearly been up in his apartment with him... especially since neither of those things had ever occurred before.

"Move along," he told them, ushering them down the stairs before they could ask questions. They made their way out to the rear parking lot, and joined the small cluster of employees and construction workers who'd left from the other exits.

Donnie reached into his back pocket for his cell and called Villi, who answered on the first ring. "Tell me you're inside the building right now shutting this thing down, man," he demanded over the sound of the alarm.

"Ah, shit. The alarm again? I leave the building for one

minute to walk down the street and grab a coffee, and you light the place on fire?" Villi joked.

Donnie was not amused.

"I'm about done with this shit, man," Donnie told him, wrapping his arm around Grace's shoulders as a chilly breeze from the nearby harbor blew over them. "You'd better drop the coffee and *hustle*."

"We're hurrying," the other man agreed, before yelling at his assistant. "Come on, Gib!" Then to Donnie, he explained, "I already started working on the problem. Looks like there's a malfunctioning sensor above the stairway, and I've gotta order a replacement. Might take a day? Two at the most. Got us disconnected from the central system temporarily, so at least you won't have sirens rolling down the street."

"Is that legal?" Donnie demanded.

"Of course!" Villi said, annoyed that Donnie would suggest anything else. "You're not required to be hooked up to the system. You *are* required to still have the alarms, which obviously you do."

"Obviously," Donnie agreed dryly. "Since they'll be ringing in my damn ears until you get back here."

"Right," Villi confirmed apologetically. "Listen, I'll walk you through the system today, and show you how you can reset it yourself in case it happens again."

Donnie pulled Grace more closely into his body and sighed as he disconnected and slid his phone into his back pocket.

"Villi will be here any minute," he told Andy and Connie. "And he knows we need this fixed *yesterday*."

"Another false alarm?" Andy asked, pushing his hand through his sandy hair.

"I don't see smoke, so it seems pretty likely," Donnie

confirmed. "And Villi says he's been working on the system. But let's give him a chance to check it out before we go back in. Besides, it's even louder inside."

Andy nodded. He'd grabbed the clipboard from Connie and now tapped his pen against it, studiously avoiding looking at Grace, who had wrapped her arm around Donnie's waist and burrowed her face into his chest. Connie didn't hold back. She pushed her dyed-black hair over her shoulder, glanced meaningfully at Grace, and raised an eyebrow at Donnie expectantly.

Donnie smiled. "Con, Andy, this is Grace. She's…" He hesitated for just a moment as vocabulary failed him. What *was* Grace to him, exactly? Guest, friend, girlfriend, submissive? He shrugged and hit on the truest, simplest thing. "She's mine."

"Yours?" Connie repeated skeptically, but Donnie paid no attention. Grace's arm had tightened around his waist and she lifted her head to give him a blinding smile that made his gut clench with need.

Damn the alarm, he wanted to get her back inside immediately. He blew out a breath and made himself finish, "Grace, this is Connie and this is Andy."

Grace exchanged smiles and nods with each of the others. Connie, correctly sensing that Donnie would not be giving her any additional information about Grace, excused herself to go and chat with some members of the cleaning crew.

"Well, hey again, stranger," another, all-too-familiar voice said from behind him.

Donnie turned his head to find Julie breaking away from the other group, just as Connie joined them.

Julie. Christ. That's just what he needed.

But as Julie got closer, he saw that she wasn't looking at *him* at all. Her attention, and her wide, warm smile, were focused on Grace. A shiver of unease worked its way up his spine.

"Honey, you look *chilly*," Julie told Grace in concern.

What the hell? When had Grace and Julie ever spoken? Unless Grace had strayed from the apartment again, after he'd spanked her and… He felt a spurt of anger in his belly. The woman knew better than to disobey him, but he'd be happy to give her another lesson in natural consequences.

"Oh, hey! Julie, right?" Grace said, returning Julie's smile. "Gosh, you're working again already? Late at night and early in the morning, too? Doesn't this guy ever let you leave?" She smiled up at Donnie, and then frowned uncertainly as she caught sight of his face.

"When did you two meet?" Donnie asked. He could hear the thread of displeasure in his voice, and saw Andy frown in his direction, but didn't care. He wanted the truth from Grace.

"L-last night," Grace said, staring up at him in concern. "You sent me up to the apartment while you checked your email, and Julie was still working. We passed in the hall, and she said she liked my jeans." Grace shrugged and gave Julie another small smile. "I told her I'd take her shopping sometime and show her how to find the bargains."

Julie nodded.

Grace's explanation was matter-of-fact and absolutely believable, but it did nothing to quell his sense of disquiet. Something about the situation seemed *off*. The hand not wrapped around Grace's waist clenched into a fist as Donnie turned to glare at Julie. "And what were you doing here last night?" he growled.

Julie licked her lips nervously, and seemed to cower before him. "A-andy asked me to come and check all the supplies in the restrooms and demo rooms. He wanted me to inventory the stockroom, too, so that he could place an order today. But I had a doctor's appointment yesterday, so he said it was okay if I went last night," she whispered, clearly upset by Donnie's tone.

Andy stepped forward to put protective hand on Julie's shoulder. Though he was several inches shorter than Donnie, he was stocky and muscular, and his hazel eyes narrowed as he glared at Donnie. "That's right," Andy soothed Julie, before telling Donnie, "If you have a problem with her being here last night, blame *me*, boss."

Donnie sighed and rubbed the back of his neck. Mikey and Salazar, Grace reappearing and dredging up ghosts from his past; it had all set him on edge. Now he was jumping at shadows. *Shit.* Yeah, so he'd gotten a weird vibe from Julie in the past… some unrequited crush of hers. But he'd told Julie the score, laid it out for her straight. Had he been misreading the situation? Had he been misconstruing her eager, helpful attitude for something more sinister? Were his instincts that *off*?

He shook his head at himself and squeezed Grace's waist, just as the breeze kicked up again, making Grace shudder.

"I apologize, Julie," Donnie said. "This alarm is bugging the crap out of me. Not your fault."

She nodded and gave him a brilliant smile, then turned to smile at Grace. "I have a sweatshirt in my car," she offered, nodding at a small blue Ford parked just a few feet away. "I think it'll fit you."

"Villi should have this turned off in no time," Donnie began, but Grace glanced up at him again and bit her lip hopefully.

"But in the meantime, maybe I could just borrow her sweatshirt?" Grace pleaded.

The wind was ruffling Grace's long hair, and goose bumps had broken out across her arms.

"Yeah," he agreed. "That'd be great. Thanks, Julie."

Julie beamed with pleasure and held out a hand for Grace, who unlatched herself from Donnie's side and followed. The place where Grace had pressed against him felt chilly and empty and he had to force himself to stuff his hand in his pocket and look away from her.

"What's up with that?" Andy asked, nodding toward Grace.

Donnie shrugged. "Grace is an old friend. We recently got reacquainted, and now we're together."

Andy shook his head and scowled. "Yeah, great. I'm happy for you, man. But I meant what the fuck is up with the way you're treating *Julie*. She's been a godsend; you know? She works a million hours unpaid, she's always looking to take on more responsibility, she's great with customers and happy to demo when we need her to, and she's a total sweetheart! Every single day, she's up on the third floor, bringing the construction guys iced coffee and pastries, swapping stories with them on their breaks. The other day, she was down on the floor with one of the electricians, helping him install something. She'd build the place up from scratch for you, if you asked her to. She's eager to please."

Inside the building, the fire alarm cut off sharply, and everyone in the parking lot breathed a sigh of relief as they shuffled back inside.

Donnie was momentarily stunned. He'd never had a problem with Andy in the past, but he wouldn't tolerate the other man's defensiveness when Donnie had done nothing more than question an employee. Clearly Julie had managed to wrap the man around her finger.

"Listen, I know you mean well," Donnie told Andy, eyes narrowed in warning. "But security is a very real issue at The

Club. I'd prefer that employees stick to their regularly scheduled shifts, or at the very least, that you email me to let me know a change has been made."

Andy looked immediately contrite. "Yeah. Yeah, I shoulda sent you an email. Sorry, Don. Just... remember Julie's a good kid, okay?"

Donnie nodded and clapped a hand on Andy's shoulder as the man walked into the building. But as he held out a hand and watched Grace jog the five steps across the asphalt to join him again, he saw a look pass over Julie's face that wasn't entirely friendly... and he knew that, whether he was overreacting or not, he would not be leaving Grace alone with her again.

"So, what do you think?" Donnie asked Grace, as they stood on the beach across the street from The Club and watched the moonlight dance on the water.

"Think about what?" Grace returned quietly. She settled her head back against Donnie's shoulder, and he tightened his arms around her waist, pulling her back more fully against his chest. He ran his nose along the column of her throat, inhaling the scent of cinnamon sugar and fresh ocean breeze, and loving the way she trembled against him.

"Think about your birthday, baby. I'm pretty sure we've celebrated the hell out of it," he told her, making her chuckle softly.

"Best ever, thanks to you," she confirmed softly, and he felt a knot in his chest loosen. Grace had been quiet and contemplative all afternoon, and he knew something had been weighing on her mind. Their relationship was new, even if their friendship was old, and he knew it would take time for her to instinctively turn to him when something was wrong. Still, it eased something inside him to know that whatever was bothering her, it didn't seem to be regrets about the way they'd spent the day.

Once he'd sorted the situation with Villi, including a quick rundown on the alarm system that he hoped he'd never need, he and Grace had jumped on the bike. They'd mostly stayed local, eating fried seafood and drinking blueberry beer at a dive bar just over the Fore River Bridge before cruising back to town to get a huge slice of the tres leches cake he knew Grace would adore from the little bakery he'd found. Donnie had parked his bike next to the beach and they'd left their shoes behind on the pavement above as they carried their cake down the wide stone steps to the sand. The sand was too cold to sit on this early in the year, so they'd eaten the cake standing up, leaning against the sea wall, and Donnie had taken great pleasure in forking enormous, messy bitefuls into her mouth, just so he could lean over and lick her lips clean.

She was sweeter than the frosting.

"You ready to go home?" he asked, settling his mouth at the juncture of her neck and shoulder. His breath made her shiver, and she tilted her head to the side, giving him better access. He ran his teeth over the tendon there, and her breathing changed, coming faster now.

His Gracie was aroused.

The urge came over him to *bite* her there, to mark her, but before his instinct got the better of him, he pulled away. Grace sighed.

"Well…" she said. "I was thinking that the birthday's not over yet."

He smirked. "I s'pose you have a few hours left," he allowed.

"Yeah, but I mean, we haven't covered all the things on your birthday celebration list," she told him. "I had my spanking. I had my drink. I had my cake…"

Her voice was low and threaded with desire. She wrapped her hands around his wrists where they rested at her waist and pulled them up slowly until his hands were just below her breasts. He felt his cock spring to life as a powerful wave of lust rolled through him.

It amazed him that he'd never allowed himself to think of Grace this way over the years, never allowed himself to imagine them together in a sexual way. Somehow, in just a few short days, wanting her had become as natural and as vital to him as oxygen. Right now, he couldn't imagine *not* wanting her.

The knowledge that *she* wanted *him* nearly as much made his breath catch.

He widened his stance in the sand as much as his jeans would allow, mitigating their height difference, and pushed his cock against her lush, round ass.

"*Fuck*," he hissed, lifting his hand to cup her breasts, and weighing them in his palms as she moaned loudly. "You did *not* wanna start this here, baby. You shoulda waited until we were back in my nice comfortable bed."

"No," she told him, shaking her head. "I shouldn't."

She reached her hand around to cup the back of his neck and pulled his head down to her shoulder. "Bite me, Donnie," she begged, her voice nearly a whimper. "Right here."

He ground himself against her again, rolling his hips as pleasure spiked through him. "No, angel," he told her. "I'm not going to hurt you. Not like this."

"Please, Donnie!" She turned her head, and in the moonlight he saw that her eyes were shining with love and trust… and need. "God, *please*."

He swallowed hard, trying to remember why this wasn't a good idea. Grace... he *couldn't* hurt her. He needed to protect her. He needed to take care of her.

He didn't realize he'd said the words aloud until Grace turned to face him, wrapping her arms around his neck and threading her fingers through his hair.

"If you want me, and you want to take care of me, *please* don't hold back with me, Donnie. That's the worst thing you could do."

He shook his head and clamped his hands on her hips, holding her immobile, even as vicious longing thrummed through his body, nearly overwhelming his caution. "You don't know what you're asking."

"Someone told me recently that there are two types of girls, Donnie. The girls men *fall in love with* and the girls men *fuck*. Is that true?" Her eyes narrowed, her hot breath lashed his cheek, and his hands clenched involuntarily at the way her full lips looked as she pronounced the word *fuck*. Then the meaning of her words penetrated the haze over his mind.

"Who said that?" he demanded, holding her steady as she tried to pull herself against him.

"Doesn't matter. Is it *true*? Is it wrong for me to want things with you? Things I... things I've only read about? Things I've wanted to try? I was a virgin until this morning, but that doesn't mean that I haven't thought about it. Dreamed about it. Do you only want me if I'm some pure, sweet, virginal little—"

"No!" he told her, stung by her words. "Christ, no. I've wanted you from the second I laid eyes on you in that tiny little bed at Joe's. I could barely keep my hands off you, even then, and every minute since has been... torture."

She shook her head impatiently. "Then you've gotta see that

I'm not a little girl anymore. I haven't been for a long time. I've been dealing with *mi mama*, and Pedro, and Mikey, and all that bullshit for years. Running the household, holding down a job. I *love* that you want to take care of me, and God, I *want* you to do that. I like having you in control. But I don't need to be locked in an ivory tower. I don't need to be protected from my own desires or *yours*, because… That's not safety, it's suffocation."

"You're wrong," he said, the words rough and heavy. "It's not about girls you fall in love with and girls you fuck. I don't even know what that means. There is only one girl I've ever fallen in love with, Grace Diaz, and if you think I don't want to fuck you every minute of the day, you're crazy." He lowered his head and bit her bottom lip hard enough to make her moan, and his hands slid around to cup her ass. "But I don't want to do anything that would harm this… *us*. I don't want to fuck this up."

She pressed herself against him, and he could feel the stiff peaks of her nipples rubbing against his chest, even through their clothing. He bit back a groan.

"If you want me, the *real* me, you can't put me on a pedestal," she whispered. "Believe me when I tell you what I want and what I *need*. And if you want this thing we have growing between us to last? Then you've got to show me the real you, and trust that I can handle what *you* need, too."

Donnie sucked in a breath and lifted his hand to cup her cheek. The wind whipped her long hair around his arm, tethering them together.

"And what do you want, Grace?" he demanded.

She stared at him, unflinching.

"I want *all* of it. Every kinky thing you've ever done to another girl, I want you to do with me. Every dirty fantasy you've ever had in the dark of night that made you blush in the morning, everything you've ever tried to convince yourself that you *shouldn't* want, that no nice girl would ever want, I want you to unleash on *me*. I want you to tie me up, strap me down, and show me how very, very good it can feel to *hurt*."

Her words were a match that set fire to his blood. His cock strained against his jeans, his pulse beat a furious tempo in his brain. *That* was what she wanted? What she needed?

Nothing in life had ever come easily to Donnie. He'd never gotten anything that he didn't have to fight and bleed for, and suddenly this woman, *his* woman, was saying that his every twisted fantasy was his for the taking… that he could have the beauty and the glory of Grace, and every depraved thing he craved, as well? He couldn't make sense of it.

She simply didn't understand what she was asking for.

But he'd show her.

He grabbed her wrists roughly, yanking them down from his neck, then twisted them high behind her back, forcing her up on her toes. She whimpered, and he felt a frisson of satisfaction at the sound.

"You want this, Grace? You want me rough?"

"Yes," she said defiantly. "*Yes!*"

"When you've had enough, you say *Stop*. But until then… here's your first lesson." He moved even closer, so his words were a whisper in her ear. "Have you ever gone down on a man, Grace? Ever sucked a cock between those lips?"

He was pretty confident she hadn't, but with his cheek pressed against hers, he could feel the heat rise to her face and knew she was blushing hard.

When she didn't respond, he tugged harder on her wrist, forcing a cry from her. "Answer me," he told her.

"N-no."

With his free hand, he gripped her jaw lightly but firmly. "Tonight, you'll call me Master Nolan."

She swallowed, and her eyes widened further. She licked her lips. "Yes, Master Nolan."

Christ. The words threatened to send the red haze over his vision that always preceded a loss of control, but he beat it back.

"I'm going to force you to your knees, Grace," he told her conversationally, brushing his thumb roughly across her bottom lip. "And you're going to suck me off. Right here. Where anyone could see us."

Her breath hit his damp finger in shallow pants, and he wasn't sure if it was arousal or fear that had her breathless... but she didn't say *Stop*, so he told himself he didn't care. He was waiting for her to call his bluff. Any minute now, she'd tell him she'd had enough...

"Yes, Master Nolan."

Fuck.

He released her hands and pushed her down until her knees hit the cold, damp sand. "Grip your hands together behind your back," he commanded.

He carefully unzipped his jeans and pushed down his boxers, allowing his rock-hard erection to spring free. Once again, he spread his legs, lining his cock up with the height of her lips. "Open."

Her eyes were dark liquid fire that burned in the moonlight, and her cheeks nearly glowed with heat as her mouth opened for him obediently.

The first warm, moist breath that passed her lips had a drop of pre-cum beading at his slit, and despite the near-darkness, he saw her fascinated gaze lock there. Without prompting, her tongue darted out to lick it off.

"Jesus, Grace."

Any chance that he might have had to call this off, any dim idea in his mind that this was just a test and he wouldn't make her go through with it, receded with that first touch.

He needed to *own* that pretty mouth.

"Suck it," he told her gruffly. And then, because he couldn't help himself, he wound her long, silky hair around his hands and guided her head forward.

His entire body seized, muscles locking down, as she sucked the tip in first. She was hesitant and cautious, and it hit him again that he was the first man to ever use her this way. He felt himself grow harder.

"You keep that mouth open, Grace," he warned her. "And when I let go, you swallow me down."

Her eyes. *Fuck*, those eyes. She was afraid, but she trusted him. And she wanted this as much as he did. That was enough to make him loose the reins.

He pushed himself forward, holding her in place as he slid into the wet furnace of her mouth and the head of his cock touched the back of her throat. Part of him screamed to push harder, to fuck her face and thrust himself down her throat until she gagged and choked. But then her cheeks hollowed out as she sucked him hard, distracting him.

As he pulled away, her tongue swirled against the underside of him. His fingers clenched in her hair reflexively and she groaned around him. The connection he felt to her was beyond anything he'd ever experienced.

"God, angel."

He'd participated in a million scenes over the years, fucked dozens of women, but none had ever been like this. Every slide, every thrust, every moan and catch of her breath, reminded him that she was there for *him*, on her knees for *him and only him*. Nothing had ever felt so good.

Within minutes... fucking *minutes*... he could feel his balls tightening and he picked up his pace, fucking her mouth with short but brutal thrusts. She gagged, but then hummed in pleasure, and the vibration of her lips around him had him nearly at the edge.

"*I'm close,*" he warned.

He could feel that her eyes were watering as beads of moisture ran down her cheeks and collected on his thumbs, but she didn't make a single noise of objection, she simply sucked harder. Her eyes lifted to meet his, incandescent with arousal, and she undulated her body as though seeking friction. Christ, was she wet from sucking him? From being used this way?

On that thought, he exploded, his cum shooting down her throat as he cried out her name. After a single, startled, choked breath, she swallowed, and then swallowed again, until she'd taken every last drop. While his chest heaved like a bellows, her tongue darted out to lick the last bits of semen from his cock.

"Oh, angel," he said hoarsely. "The way you look on your knees with your mouth on me, the way you swallowed me down, the way you cleaned me up so prettily...You're so fucking dirty, and so fucking *amazing*."

He lifted her to her feet and pressed his lips to hers, feeling a possessive thrill when he tasted himself on her tongue. He wrapped his arms around her, cradling her like she was the most precious thing in his world.

Because she was.

He pulled back a moment later and watched her carefully. Her lips were swollen and darker, her cheeks were flushed, and her eyes were damp, but she held his gaze, and then she smiled, wide and happy. *Proud.*

"You liked that, didn't you?" he murmured. "You liked having me fuck your face, letting me use you like that?"

"You don't scare me, baby," she whispered. "I want this. I want you. Because, Donnie? When you've shown me all of your fantasies and all of your darkness? When I've shown you that I love every corner of you, even the parts you're not proud of? Then you'll be *mine*… the way that I have *always* been yours."

He shook his head in disbelief. God, his woman undid him.

He wanted what she promised. And all he needed to do to have this was to rid himself of every preconceived notion of how he *should* act with her, talk to her openly and listen to her cues, and trust that she would be honest about her limits. It was a basic idea. The kind of Dominant Training 101 shit that he was *paid* to teach others, but somehow it was harder when it was Grace.

He opened his eyes and nodded.

"Come on," he told her shortly. "You have a few more hours of birthday left, and I know exactly how I want you to spend them."

Chapter 8

Half caught in the enchantment somewhere between waking and sleeping, Grace sighed with contentment as she woke. No. No, this wasn't a dream. Neither had her birthday, the day before, been a dream. She was pressed up against Donnie's warm, bare chest, his arm tucked around her waist, his huge hand flat against her belly. She was warm and content, the strength and protection of the man she loved as comforting as the blanket over her. She'd never pegged Donnie as the spooning type, but had he ever proven her wrong. After a full day of birthday festivities, she'd collapsed into bed exhausted, and for the first time since he'd taken her to his apartment, he'd joined her.

It had been the best birthday of her life, better even than the one time in her childhood she ever remembered her mama throwing a party where Grace got to invite her friends from school. They'd had a piñata, and games, and she'd gotten so many birthday presents she couldn't see over the top of the pile. She remembered that birthday for years, but it paled in comparison to spending the day with Donnie. She squirmed. *Everything* paled in comparison to taking his cock and sucking him off as his eyes went half-lidded on the beach.

"You awake, angel?" His deep voice, still gritty from sleep, made her spine tingle.

"Mmmm," she said, twisting around to him. When he lifted his arm, she crawled in, nestling her head on his chest while he held her, hitching up her knee against the length of his long, muscled legs. She shivered. He was delicious. "I'm awake," she said. "But I don't want to move. This is too nice."

He chuckled, one hand traveling down to her ass and squeezing. "Is it?" he said. "Cuz I can think of a few ways it can get a whole lot nicer."

And just like that, her breasts swelled, her pussy throbbed, and she tingled with excitement. He yawned, as she watched his sleepy brown eyes focus on hers, smiling at her. His long blond hair was tousled on the pillow. Running a finger along the scruff on his jaw, she smiled softly to herself.

"Oh yeah?" she teased. "How so?"

He grinned. Flat-out *grinned*. "You could go make me some coffee and some breakfast."

"Donnie!" she poked his belly, and his hand nabbed her wrist.

"No poking," he said, growing sober. She shot him a mock glare, but he raised an eyebrow, and she felt the responding thump of her heart.

"You can tease me but I can't poke you?"

"You can tease me back," he said, still grasping her wrist. "But don't poke me."

She couldn't help herself. "Oh yeah?" she teased. "And what'll happen if I do?"

He sobered even further, pushed himself up, and before she

knew what was happening, he was on top of her, straddling her, both of her wrists pinned helplessly as she squirmed beneath him. His mouth came to her ear. "Do you need a reminder, Gracie? Of what happens to you if you don't do what you're told?"

Did she? She wasn't sure if he was teasing or serious, and she wasn't sure where the line was, how far she could tease and what would get her for real tossed over his knee. "I… um… am not sure," she said.

He laughed out loud but didn't release her wrists.

"Then allow me to clarify," he said. "You want to disobey me, give it a go, angel, and you'll find yourself over my lap. Talk back to me, and I'll spank you." He sobered and fixed her with a stern look. "You put yourself in danger, and I'll take my belt to your ass. Got it?"

Her panties dampened, and her stomach clenched. She swallowed, and nodded. "Yeah," she whispered. "I understand."

Bending down so that his breath tickled her cheek, his knees pressed up against her, her whole body shivered in anticipation. His mouth came to her ear and he whispered, "You sure, Grace? You sure you can handle this? Because this is who I am. Doms protect and doms like control. I'll be gentle with you, but I need to know you're in this because you want to be, not because you don't want to let me down."

He was holding himself back, this much she knew. He hadn't held back the night before, and she'd *loved* it. She wanted to be owned by him, used by him. There was more to all of this than he'd let on. Yes, he'd spanked her, and she knew without a shadow of a doubt that if he decided she needed another spanking, he wouldn't hesitate to take his hand to her ass. And though the thought of being punished was a tad bit scary, she had always known Donnie was a guy who needed to be in control. Even though she couldn't understand it herself, the thought of being spanked or punished by him—hell, *especially* being punished—gave her a thrill of excitement. She didn't get all of it yet, but she knew she liked what he gave her. She knew she trusted him with her life.

"Donnie," she whispered back. "I don't even know what 'this' is, but if you mean am I okay with you being a dom? Then, honey, the answer is, yeah. You've been a dom since you were like fifteen."

He chuckled, his mouth coming to her ear. She gasped as he pulled the lobe into his mouth and gently nipped. "I'll show you what 'this' is," he said. "Slowly. I'll be gentle."

She moaned. "I hope not too gentle."

His tongue flicked out and tasted where he'd nipped. Her wrists still held in his strong grasp, helpless beneath him, she pushed back but he held tight. She wriggled, wanting him to touch her, *needing* his hand between her legs. She groaned. "Oh, God," she said.

"I don't know what you can handle yet, Grace," he said.

"I don't know either," she said honestly. "But there's only one way to find out."

He lifted his head, his eyes meeting hers with a possessive heat she felt straight to her pussy. His mouth came to hers and she sighed into his kiss. God, he tasted so good. The barest flick of his tongue against hers had her squirming, the firm feel of his erection pressed up against her belly fueling her own desire. She made him hard, and she fucking loved that she did.

Buzzz.

Donnie froze, and Grace followed suit. What was that noise?

Buzzz.

His phone.

"Just ignore it," she begged.

"Can't," he said with a sigh, releasing her, as he grabbed the phone and glanced at the screen. "*Fuck.*"

She sat up, ignoring the lump in her throat, trying hard to be a big girl but wanting no more than to spend the entire morning in bliss. How much longer could their time together last?

He nabbed the phone, climbing out of bed as he answered it. "Yeah?"

As he walked out of the room, she pushed out of bed and stomped out of his bedroom to grab a towel to take a shower. If he was going to just *leave* her like that, *fine*, she'd just do her own thing. But as she rounded the corner, nearing where he was talking on the phone, she felt her t-shirt snagged from behind. She whirled. Donnie towered over her, his eyes dark and sober. He released her t-shirt, and pointed one finger to the loveseat.

Sit, he mouthed.

Folding her arms across her chest, she stared at him, not quite willing to just do what he said, but not quite bold enough to defy him. His brows rose, and he spoke into his phone. "Slay, give me a sec." He took the phone from his ear, hit what she could only assume was the "mute" button, placing his phone on the arm of the loveseat. Uh oh.

Donnie grabbed her upper arm, spun her around, and delivered one sharp, pointed swat.

"Sit," he ordered, pointing again.

This time, she obeyed, no longer feeling quite as petulant, and more than a little subdued.

No fair.

But as she sat on the couch, she raked her eyes over him. He stood in nothing but his boxers, quite the sight to behold. The muscles on his arms bunched as he lifted one arm and ran his fingers through his long, sandy hair. "Got it," he said. "Yeah, I'll look into it. Thanks, man. Yeah, see you tonight."

He hit a button on his phone, placed it down, and gave Grace one long, stern stare. She shrank into the loveseat.

"Important call?" she said sheepishly, with what she hoped was her most innocent expression.

He stalked to her, the tips of his lips quirking up as he drew closer and she attempted to squish further back on the couch.

She slowly got to her feet, sidestepping him, and covering her ass with the towel she'd managed to grab. "I'm just going to, um, make my way to the shower, and then I'll—ahhhhhhhh!"

She screamed as he pounced, lifting her straight up in the air, sitting down on the couch, and pulling her on his lap so that she straddled him.

"Not yet you're not," he said.

She cleared her throat. "Alrighty then."

"I had to take that call. Even though we've had a… leisurely morning here, I can't slack off of my duties." His look was sober now, stern even, and the mere look made a zing of arousal shoot straight through her. She squirmed uncomfortably on his lap, as she felt his hardness beneath her. He reached his hand to the back of her neck, entwined his fingers in her hair, and pulled, the sensation sharp but erotic, little tingles of pain and pleasure making her shiver. His mouth came to her ear as he pulled her toward him. "As much as I want to fuck you until you can't remember your name or what day it is, it'll have to wait. But I promise the wait will be worth your while." She stopped breathing entirely as his free hand slowly grazed the front of her t-shirt, the pad of his thumb gliding over her taut nipple. "So you have two choices," he continued to whisper in her ear. "Either you'll go take your shower now and I'll take you to get some breakfast, or you give me lip and I'll whip your ass."

God!

"What'll it be, angel?"

She hesitated a moment too long. He released her hair, and his palm cracked down on her backside, reminding her that as hot as getting her ass whipped *sounded*, being on the receiving end of a spanking from Donnie was still very *painful*. She nearly leapt off his lap and ran to the bathroom, calling over her shoulder. "Option A, and I need coffee!"

As the stream of water hit her back seconds later, she could still hear him chuckling.

"Oh, Donnie. Oh, it's beautiful," Grace breathed, as she took off the full face helmet he'd made her wear. She hadn't wanted to wear it, but at the twitching muscle in his jaw, she'd slammed it on her head, muttering the whole time.

They parked the bike, and walked together to get some breakfast sandwiches and coffee, before he took her to a secluded picnic area by the beach. It was still chilly on the beach in early May with the Boston heat still several months out. She shivered as he handed her the steaming styrofoam mug, and she sat on the picnic bench. He shrugged out of his coat and placed the heavy, warm leather jacket over her shoulders.

"I'm fine, Donnie," she said, not wanting him to be without his own jacket, but he merely lifted a brow. She quieted, and focused on unwrapping her sandwich.

She was learning.

"Yeah, I like it here," he said. "Not a lot of people come here on weekdays." He liked quiet and solitude, she was beginning to realize, gravitating to where it was quiet, and he could be left alone. "You like your sandwich?"

Nodding appreciatively, she took another bite of the sausage-egg wrap. It was perfectly seasoned, with creamy cheese and flecks of peppers, reminding her of her mama's *huevo el plato*, a savory egg dish she'd grown up with.

"Love it," she said, taking a sip of coffee. "Hey, what was up with Slay earlier this morning?"

Donnie shrugged, taking a sip from his own cup. He'd already eaten half his sandwich in two bites, and was now looking out at the ocean as waves gently glided to shore, foamy white flecks dancing like sprinkles atop an ice cream cone. "Looks like everything's going ahead with Chalo's release later today. This time tomorrow, he'll be a free man. But don't worry, Grace, we still have things we're working on."

Grace nodded thoughtfully. What would happen when the men who'd planned on using her found that she was missing? Would Donnie and his friends be able to find out what they needed to in time? She hated the unknown, worrying about her mama, and even Pedro. He was such an asshole and she might never forgive him, but he was her brother and she couldn't remember a time when she hadn't looked out for him. Where would she be this time next week? Really, how long could she be tucked away in Donnie's place, before someone would find her?

And when they did… what then?

Her sandwich fell to her lap as she gazed out at the ocean, remembering how much simpler things were when she was younger. Her biggest fear back then was whether or not she'd finish her sand castle before the tide came in and swept it all away. How much longer would she be held in limbo? Was her whole life to be lived like this, everything she cared for built on the edge of the seashore, destined to be swept away when the time came in?

Her eyes went to Donnie. He'd finished his sandwich and was balling up the white paper wrapper, tighter and harder than was necessary. He whipped it toward a garbage barrel a few feet away. It ricocheted off the rim and fell in.

"Score," she said softly, taking another sip of coffee to help swallow the rising lump in her throat.

"Eat your sandwich, angel," Donnie said with a nod, his voice both gentle and stern. She took a small obedient bite, but her appetite had fled.

"I'm full," she said. "I don't want anymore."

He frowned disapprovingly, his lips turning down as his eyes zoned in on the half-eaten sandwich. "You haven't eaten enough," he said. "Don't tell me you're full. You need more than that."

"You can't tell me to eat," she retorted, suddenly irritated with his high handedness, her fears setting her on edge, causing her to snap. "Is this what you're like with all your girls? You make them all eat?" Her hands shook, as she placed the sandwich in her lap and met his eyes.

His eyes narrowed on hers. "All my girls?" he said, with a humorless laugh. "I only have *one* girl, and fuck yeah, I'm like this. I'll tell her when she needs to eat, and when she needs to get her ass in bed, and make sure she doesn't do dumbass shit that could get her hurt in any way." He paused a beat. "Yeah, Gracie. This is what I'm like. Now eat your goddamned sandwich."

Though her heart stuttered, and, in her mind, she knew she was acting like a spoiled brat, she couldn't seem to help it. She *hated* feeling out of control, both afraid she'd never get back what was precious to her and never keep hold of what she'd wanted her whole life. It was all too fleeting and uncertain. She balled up her sandwich and lifted her hand, prepared to whip it across the table and onto the sandy beach in front of them, like a toddler on the verge of a tantrum.

But as her hand raised, Donnie merely leveled a narrow-eyed gaze on her. "Do it," he growled. "Go ahead, babe. You want to sit on a sore ass on the back of my bike, you throw that."

The choice was an easy one as she met his gaze. Sitting on the back of his bike already hurt her ass, and the thought of being draped over his knee in broad daylight in public was enough to make her re-think her actions. The sandwich dropped to her lap as his eyes remained fixed on hers.

"Eat it, Grace," he said, his voice deeper and commanding as he stood. "Two more bites, angel."

Two more bites. She hadn't been cajoled into eating anything since she was in kindergarten. Her eyes fixed on his, she peeled back the crinkly paper, lifted the sandwich to her lips, and took a large bite. She chewed, then swallowed, intentionally licking her lips as he watched. His Adam's apple bobbed, but his brow remained furrowed, until she took not two, but several deliberate bites, polishing off the remains of her sandwich as he watched every chew and swallow.

Slowly, his narrowed eyes softened, and his lips turned up. "Good girl," he said softly, walking over to her. "That's my girl."

Warmth spread across her chest and between her thighs at the praise. God, she loved his voice. *Loved* it. Some women would fantasize about being kissed, or felt up, or fucked, and yes, she loved all of that, but she found herself fantasizing about surprisingly different things.

"What's on your mind, Gracie?" he asked, taking her

wrapper from her hand and whipping it toward the barrel. Again, a score.

"Oh, nothing," she said. It was embarrassing, and she didn't want to tell him.

"Grace," he warned, a brow raising as he crossed his arms.

"Well," she said, not wanting him to grow stern again. "I just… well, do you remember how you used to read to me?"

His eyes warmed, his lips tipped up, and the white of his teeth flashed against tanned skin as he smiled at her.

"Forgot all about that," he said. "What was it? Shakespeare or some shit, right?"

"Chaucer," she laughed. "I had to read it for English, and didn't want to, and my mama said I couldn't go to the dance unless I read it. Remember?"

She remembered…

Grace sat, scowling, on her balcony, gazing out as the sun settled behind the row of two and three-story houses, so little space between them in the inner city, that once the sun dropped, the light would be gone quickly, so she always stopped and watched it right before it vanished. The familiar growl of a motorcycle captured her attention, though, as Donnie pulled his bike to the parking space on the other side of the fence.

"Hey, Grace," he called up, lifting a hand in greeting as he swung himself off and hit the kickstand with his boot.

"Hey, Donnie," she said, her heartbeat accelerating as she saw him make sure the coast was clear before he hopped the fence. Was he coming up to their apartment? It was risky, knowing her father could come home early, but it was a risk Donnie occasionally took. To make things safer, she'd go to him instead. She jumped to her feet, trotting down several flights of stairs so quickly, she nearly slammed into him on the landing.

"Whoa, honey," he said, smiling at her. "Going somewhere?"

"Just needed to get some fresh air," she said. "You?"

His brows drew together and he frowned as he took her gently by the elbow and led her out the back door to the paved back yard, where she sat on a flimsy plastic chair. He followed suit. He shrugged. "Gotta talk to Pedro about some shit," he said, lifting a chin to her book. "What are you reading?" he asked.

She sighed. "Chaucer, for English," she said, "and it's as boring as all hell."

He reached for it and took the book. "Now, Grace, you're a smart girl," he said. "Real smart. You might not like it, but you've got to use those brains God gave you. Not everyone has brains like yours, honey. Or talent."

His praise made her suddenly feel shy. She merely looked down at her hands.

"Tell you what," he said. "Will this reading go quicker if I read it to you?"

Her heart soared as she nodded eagerly. "Oh my God, yes, for sure," she said. "Please?"

Nodding, he opened the book up where the folded-down page lay, and he smiled. "All right, I might mess up a few words," he said.

She just shook her head. She didn't care, only wanting to hear his voice. She dreamed about his voice, the deep, husky sound of it calming and reassuring. And then he began. She never did hear much that night, as all she could do was listen to the deep timbre of his voice, and feel the way just the sound did strange but pleasant things to her body. God, she could listen to him read forever. After a while, he paused.

He flipped through the pages. "How much do you have to read?"

She sighed. "Twenty pages by the time mama gets home, or I can't go to the dance tomorrow night."

His eyes lifted from the book and met hers, teasing yet somehow probing

"So if I take this book, and hide it, and you don't get your homework done, I get to keep you away from all the other boys?"

Her throat constricted and she looked away, not knowing how to respond. She laughed haltingly.

"Hey, Grace, I'm just teasing," he said. "I'm way too old for you anyway."

Her nose stung, and her eyes burned with unshed tears, but he was looking through the book and didn't notice. Was it her imagination, or did he look a little... sad?

"You're not too old for me," she protested, not knowing what else to say.

He only smiled sadly, picked up the book, and kept reading.

"God, I remember," he said. "That was some truly awful shit."

She laughed out loud. "You thought so? Then why did you read it to me?"

He smiled back. "Because I was trying to help you."

His phone buzzed in his pocket, and he quickly took it out. "Gotta take this, honey."

"Okay," she said. "Hey, I really need to hit the ladies' room." The thought of sitting on his bike as they jostled through the city had her feeling near desperate, and it appeared he understood.

He answered the phone, and held a finger up to her. "Slay, just a minute." He covered the mouthpiece, frowning, but finally relenting. "You can go back to the coffee shop where we got the sandwiches, and you can run in before we hit the road again, okay?" His eyes grew serious as he seemed to realize that she would be out of his sight, but what else could he do? He couldn't very well accompany her to the ladies' room.

"I'll be fine," she said, certain that Chalo whatever-his-name-was wouldn't be hiding his cronies in a little bathroom at some local beach dive.

"Okay," he said. "Be quick about it." He nodded, turning back to his phone, and she scurried to the ladies' room.

"Hey! Grace!" Startled, Grace turned to look, only to find Julie standing by the coffee shop with a paper bag in one hand, a cup of coffee in the other. "You here with Donnie?"

Grace nodded, suddenly feeling uneasy. Was she supposed to tell people she was with Donnie? But Julie only gave her a faint smile, before turning to go. "Okay," she said. Though Grace couldn't put her finger on it, something felt off, wrong. "See you later," Julie said, waving and turning to go. Grace breathed a sigh of relief, as she made her way to the restroom. When she came out a few minutes later, she walked quickly with her head down back to join Donnie.

"Got a light, sweetheart?" Grace jumped, not realizing there was a stranger standing in the shadow of a vacated shop.

"No," she said, keeping her head down, and walking faster. The man was hooded, and though it was broad daylight, there was something about the look in his eyes that made her shiver.

"Well aren't we rude," the man said, quickening his pace.

"Leave me alone," Grace said, picking up her pace, trying to outrun him, but within seconds, she felt him grab her elbow. She yanked back and screamed, and the second she did, the man's grip loosened and she felt a *whoosh* go past her as the man was lifted bodily off the ground. Grace gasped, spinning around, covering her mouth with her hand as Donnie dragged the man down a deserted path between the buildings, and threw him against the wall.

"Donnie!" she screamed, but she knew there was no stopping him. His eyes were mere slits, his jaw set, as he delivered a vicious blow to the man's jaw. She heard the sickening sound of the man's head snapping back, of him falling to his knees. As Donnie lifted the man and kneed him in the chest, Grace could see it, the boy she grew up with, the one with a temper and a nerve strong enough to break legs. He wouldn't hold back. He'd beat the hell out of this asshole.

"You don't fucking lay hands on my woman," Donnie growled, delivering another wicked blow.

"Donnie, stop!" she begged, afraid he would gain attention on the street, and that was the last thing they needed, but Donnie ignored her, delivered one ferocious blow after another, until the man, bloodied and bruised, slumped over. Donnie grabbed the man by the front of his shirt.

"You ever fucking touch her again, I'll kill you," he said, dropping the man to the ground.

Grace felt her jaw slacken, and a wave of nausea hit her stomach, but she had no time to think, as Donnie grabbed her hand, panting but silent, and half-dragged her to the bike.

"Get on," he growled, as he flicked on his phone and held the bike as she mounted it. He slammed the helmet on her head, not so hard it hurt, but not gently, then swung his leg up and over his Valkyrie. He revved the engine, then growled into the phone. "Beat up a son of a bitch on the corner of North and Elm. He's conscious, yeah. I lost my shit." There was a pang of regret in his voice. "Yeah. Motherfucker touched Grace." His voice had hardened, and the regret suddenly evaporated.

She latched her arms around his waist as he ended the call. Pulling away from the corner, he headed out onto the street. Though part of her was sickened by the brutality, she couldn't help but feel... awed. He'd come to rescue her. He'd kick the ass of anyone who tried to hurt her. He was still, even now, her hero, even as he'd laid waste to the creep who dared to touch her... *especially* as he did. She knew he'd done his best to detach himself from his brutal upbringing, sought to control his temper and violence, and likely felt sickened himself by the way he'd snapped. But did he have regrets? She wasn't sure.

Did she?

As the sun sank low on the horizon, she sat by his window, waiting. After breakfast on the beach, he'd gone back to The Club, ordering her upstairs. He had to check on things, he'd said, but he was only gone for short periods of time throughout the afternoon and evening before he came back up, making sure she was safe and secure.

"What is it, Donnie?" she asked at one point. "I'm fine." But he refused to answer, and did she really need him to? He'd snapped. Her safety was important to him, and the moment he'd gotten the barest whiff of danger, he'd lost all control. But he couldn't lock her up and throw away the key. They had to move on. He had work to do, and he couldn't very well keep her in his pocket.

The door jangled. She knew it was late, so late that in just an hour or two, the tinges of early morning sunlight would be peeking in through the window. By now, she knew the routine, that he'd done his late night rounds and The Club was now vacated. She heard the reassuring clomping of his boots as the door shut and the lock clicked into place. She scrambled up from where she was kneeling by the window, just as he came in the room.

"You all right?" he asked. It was the first thing he'd asked every single time he'd checked on her all day long.

She sighed. "Donnie," she said, in a voice she hoped was soothing. "I'm *fine*. Really, honey. Please. Let it go."

"Let it go?" he said, running a hand through his hair as he drew closer to her. "Some motherfucker touches my woman, and I bust his ass, and you tell me to let it go?"

Her eyes fell to his hand, swollen and bruised, a red laceration across his knuckles. But as she reached for his hand, he pulled away, shaking his head. He shrugged out of his leather jacket and hung it up on a hook in the closet.

"Matteo's covering for me tonight. Slay checked in on things by the beach, and Blake's giving me the rest of the week off."

The rest of the week off?

Grace moved to his side as he sat on the bed and removed first one boot, then the other. "Like… you got in trouble?" she asked.

Scowling, he lifted his eyes to hers. "I'm not the one in trouble, babe," he said.

Her heart gave a sudden flutter, and her palms grew sweaty. "Um… what?" she asked.

He frowned. "We've got men on you. You know that." He sat up now, and crossed his arms. "Why didn't you tell me you ran into Julie right before I kicked that guy's ass?"

Oh.

"I… forgot," she faltered, suddenly feeling her pulse pick up. "I didn't know I was supposed to tell you that."

He inhaled, then exhaled, seemingly attempting to calm his temper. "Come here," he said, pointing one large finger at the bed next to him. On trembling legs, she obeyed.

Folding his hands on his knee, he gave her a stern look. "Just because I took a call didn't mean I wasn't watching. I've been too laidback letting you do things like go to the beach, even if I'm with you. Shit happens. And yeah, babe, when you see one of the few people I can count on my hand that even knows you're here, right before I kick some loser's ass for touching you, you *tell me* that shit. Yeah?"

She nodded, her mouth growing dry as her palms dampened. Swallowing, she tried to answer. "Yeah. I get it." Her voice faltered. "I—I'm sorry, Donnie."

What exactly did he mean by *trouble?* She couldn't bring herself to ask him, as he reached for her and drew her over to him.

"I don't like that part of me you saw this morning, Grace. I've worked years at getting control of my temper, and then shit like this happens, and it shakes me."

"I know, honey," she said, running a hand across his jaw in a soothing gesture that melted the pain from his eyes. "You're protective. You're fierce. That's who you are."

His eyes closed briefly. "I don't like that I'm the kind of guy who gets off on pain."

Oh *God.*

She swallowed. "What do you mean?" she asked. "You mean, the part of you that likes to… sp-spank me?"

His eyes opened, and his lips twitched. "Not just spank, angel. But yeah, Gracie. That's what I mean. I was raised to solve problems with my fists. I learned to love control. And it's all some kinda sick, twisted shit now, and I don't know where normal and healthy even fits in anymore."

She couldn't bear to see him tortured like this. Without another word, she leaned in and brought her lips to his. His response was instinctive and immediate. Wrapping his hands around her waist so tightly it hurt, he pulled her to him and kissed her back, no holds barred. Teeth and lips clashed, and his hands were gone, raking her shirt up. Pausing the kiss only briefly enough to take it totally off, he moved her so she straddled his lap, before he went back to kissing her. His warm, rough hands scraped along her naked torso, causing her to both shiver and moan into his mouth. He lifted her and laid her on the bed gently, straddling her while he kissed her.

"There's nothing wrong with control if I want this." Her heart pounded and her legs clenched as heat flared in his eyes. "And I want this, Donnie." She reached a hand out to run it along his arms, gently. "You controlled yourself today. You left. But you've been under pressure, and you're afraid. I am, too."

He leaned down and kissed her shoulder as she ran her fingers lightly along his back. Oh, God, that felt good. "But we're in this together, honey," she whispered. "I *want* to feel your control. I *like* that you protect me."

"God, you need a good session," he whispered in her ear. "You don't even know the half of it yet."

She grinned. *She* needed a good session? What even *was* "a good session?" Even though this was totally new and she *didn't* know the half of it, she suspected his demonstrations would not only be hot as fucking hell. And if he was in control again—of *her*—would it help him regain control of himself?

"Maybe it's time I learn," she said.

His mouth came to her ear, the whiskers tickling her sensitive skin, as he whispered, "Keep your hands right where I put them. You understand me?"

"Yes," she gasped, unprepared for the way his hands clenched tighter on her waist.

"That's a yes, *sir* when I give you an instruction." She felt the decided shift in every inch of her being. She'd given him the green light. And now, he was taking control.

"Yes-yes, sir," she said, a strange sensation of being little, and out of her comfort zone, overwhelmed her, but there was barely time to focus as his teeth bit down on the tender skin of her neck, not so hard it hurt, but hard enough she froze, her pulse racing. What had she just asked for? He lifted his head and moved his mouth slowly down, tracing down her neck with his tongue as her back arched and her mouth parted, until he reached her nipple. He seized the pink bud between his teeth.

She screamed and writhed, but his hands pinned her fast as he briefly released her with his mouth, only to command, "You *stay. Right. There.*"

She didn't *breathe* as he continued the torturous, delicious assault of tongue and teeth, moving from one nipple to the next, then down the valley of her belly until he reached her navel. He lapped at her naked skin, while his fingers spread her thighs apart, prying her open and plunging deep into her core. Her hips bucked and he stopped her movements with a hard, stinging smack to her thigh.

"Donnie!" she gasped, but she realized her mistake too late. He was up, the warmth of his body gone, and he was dragging her across his lap.

"Ow!" she yelped, as he spanked her hard, one swat after another taking her breath away.

"Try that again," he commanded.

"Yes, sir!" she panted. "I'm sorry, sir!" The rapid swats immediately ceased.

"Very good," he said, pushing her gently onto the bed. "Now you strip for me."

Scrambling to obey lest she feel the sting of his palm again, she pushed to standing and quickly stepped out of her jeans and panties, pushing them to the floor and kicking them aside, her eyes traveling to the length of his erection just long enough to confirm he was as hot for her as she was for him, before meeting his eyes again. All traces of humor had fled, leaving only a stern command. He was in utter control. He nodded as she stood before him, now completely naked.

"That's right, angel. Now you go and stand up against that wall." He gestured to the wall with his left hand, while with his right, he tugged at the waist of his jeans and began to unfasten his belt. She froze.

You put yourself in danger, I'll take my belt to your ass.

She realized with a quickening of her heartbeat that a muscle was ticking in his jaw.

"Yes, sir," she breathed, quickly stepping over to the wall.

"That's right, Grace. Face the wall, and place your arms above your head, palms down flat. Spread your legs."

Oh God oh God oh God.

Trembling, she obeyed, closing her eyes, the only sound in the room now the jingle of his belt, followed by the whoosh of leather through loops as he removed it. She could hear him stalking behind her now. "Are you going to be a good girl?"

"Yes, sir," she said. What would happen if she said no?

"Very good," he said. "Stand there. You'll take my belt, Grace. You won't move."

"Yes, sir," she repeated. Her pussy throbbed as the whistle of leather through air warned her a split second before the tail end of his belt lashed her. She jumped, but otherwise stayed in position. It hurt like hell, but only briefly. Seconds later, another lash fell, followed by another. The bite of leather made her squirm, and just when she thought she couldn't take another blow, she could feel him at her back, his hand at her legs, spreading them wide. His large, rough palm smoothed over the heat on her seared skin, the pain melting to warmth as he massaged her.

"How are you holding up, angel?" he whispered in her ear, as he grasped a fistful of her hair and pulled.

"I'm good," she gasped, as he tugged her hair again.

"Do you want more?"

Hell, yeah, she wanted more. "Please, sir," she said, her mouth parted as the words came strangled and desperate. "I do. I want more." She had to prove to him she could take this. Tilting her head to the side, and giving him a look from beneath lowered lashes, she licked her lips and swallowed before continuing. He liked it dirty.

She'd give him dirty.

"I'll do anything you tell me, sir. I'm yours to do with what you will."

He grinned, still tugging her hair, a fire in his eyes glowing as he pulled, dragging her back over to the bed.

"Are you a pain slut, angel?" Her heart thumped at his words, but she would not cower or desist. She *had* to show him she could take it. She nodded her head eagerly, urging him to continue. "What do you want more? My belt or my cock?"

Her body quaked in anticipation, heady from the power he wielded over her, and the erotic pull of submitting to his every salacious whim. "Both," she breathed. His eyes never left hers as he slowly placed the belt on the bed, grabbing the edge of his t-shirt as he pulled it off, his hardened muscles bunching until he sat in front of her, bare-chested. He took the shirt and pulled it taut, leaning down, as he slipped the warm, white fabric over her eyes. It was soft and smelled deliciously like him. As her world plunged into darkness, arousal flared through her.

He was near enough for her to hear, but she couldn't see what he was doing. Slave only to the sensation of smell and touch, she shivered as his hands ran down the length of her body, from the tops of her shoulders down her arms, stroking firmly, possessively. Her breath came in pants as he drew a finger between her folds, which were damp with arousal.

"Fucking hell," he growled in her ear. "You're soaked, angel." He drew his finger upward, past her mound, and further up, until he reached her breasts. Both hands were on her nipples now, pinching and twisting.

"Ow!" she protested, but his firm grasp didn't slacken. He twisted, not so hard it was unbearable, but enough that she squirmed in discomfort.

"Donnie!"

"You'll learn to like this, Gracie."

Would she?

He released her, and when she was no longer held by the pain, a rush of warmth and tingling sensation of electric arousal pulsed through her.

Maybe she would.

A *whizz* of a zipper, then her head was being pulled back by another hard tug of hair. "You'll take me in your mouth now," he said. "And suck me off while I whip your ass."

Ohhhh *God*.

"Yes, sir," she said, not knowing what else to do but wait, on her knees, plunged into darkness by the makeshift blindfold, for his command. His hand was on her cheek, guiding her, as she felt the tip of his cock on her lips just as she had last night. A delicious wave of his power and arousal made her lightheaded, the anticipation nearly unbearable. She flicked her tongue out and connected with soft, warm skin, hearing the breath hiss out of him. Taking him fully in her mouth, she began to suckle and tease, seconds before she heard the now-familiar jingle of his belt buckle, a *whizz*, and a crack as pain blossomed across her ass. She held his cock firm in her mouth, not releasing him, as he lashed her again, hard enough to sting but soft enough she felt little more than a warm, delicious fire building. Swat after swat landed as she sucked him, pumping his cock with one hand while she worked her tongue over his tip, alternating sucks and licks.

He groaned, but didn't let up on the spanking, one lash after another falling as she sucked, fully immersed in pleasing him while he whipped her into submission. She could feel him tensing, near climax, when he dropped his belt and withdrew his cock, lifting her up in his arms. He planted her face-down on the bed, still blindfolded with his t-shirt, arranging her so she was chest-down and ass up, her arms in front of her like a supplicant.

"Gonna take this pussy," he rumbled.

"Yes, sir," she said, loving the way it felt to call her hero *sir*, something special and wicked, and arousing. His hands planted on either side of her hips, and she could feel the head of his cock at her entrance.

"Tell me, angel," he said, softer now. "Tell me if I hurt you."

"I will," she whispered, and then he was in her, and she was filled with him, his cock throbbing as waves of pleasure rocked her body.

"Grace," he said, his fingers raking over her clit as he pumped into her, and *God*, was she gonna come already? He worked her over as he thrust into her, her need getting near frantic with every push. It felt different accepting him from behind like this. She felt somehow fuller, more aroused, even, and though the feel of him still stretched her with touches of pain, it was bearable, as bearable as the delicious licks of his belt had been. She wanted to *own* his pain, absorb it into her very soul.

"I love you," he said, grunting his release as she fell over the edge into ecstasy, climaxing as he rode her hard. "God, I love you."

"Yes, sir," she said when she could speak again, not knowing how to respond or if *sir* was still expected. "Donnie, I love you so much." A final thrust for him, and he collapsed, holding himself up but barely, as he withdrew and pulled her over on top of him as he removed the t-shirt from her eyes.

"Stay there, honey," he said, getting out of bed and grabbing a washcloth. He came back quickly, cleaning her up as she lay in the ecstatic afterglow. She could get used to lying here with him like this, just after being spanked and fucked senseless. Hell, she couldn't even feel her legs. As she rolled over, and he pulled her into his arms for a cuddle, she froze.

An obnoxious blare of an alarm rang in the distance.

"Fucking *hell*," Donnie growled. "I'll beat the shit out of those dumbasses if they don't get these alarms fixed."

She groaned. The last thing she needed was him leaving her right now, but it seemed he had no choice. "I'll be right back, Gracie," he promised, as he stood, pulling on a pair of jeans, grumbling to himself.

"Please," she said. "Be quick?" She needed him now. Her body still ached from the way he'd worked her over, and she needed the reassurance of his touch.

He leaned in and ran his hands through the hair at the back of her neck, his fingers claiming but gentle. "I promise, honey. I promise I'll be right back for you."

"Oh yeah?" she teased, though there was a thread of irritability in her voice. She really *didn't* want him to go. "How do you know I'll still be here when you get back?"

She'd underestimated his ability to read her, she realized, as he gave her a sidelong glance. Though his lips twitched, his eyes were serious, focused. "Oh, honey, I have ways to ensure you stay exactly where I put you."

She'd thought it wasn't possible for him to arouse her yet again, but she was wrong. Her body ached for him, and already, her clit pulsed and arousal shot through her chest. "Oh yeah?" she whispered.

In one swift move, he lifted his t-shirt from the bed. He was a big enough guy that the shirt was long enough for him to twist it into a rope, before he fastened it around her wrists. "I'll tie you to my bed if I have to," he said, securing her as he knelt next to her. He kissed her forehead, making her chest rise, before he released her. "I'll be back," he said. "It'll only take a minute. And when I come back, we'll have a talk about making sure you behave yourself." Her heart stuttered in anticipation.

"Yes, sir."

The door shut with finality.

Chapter 9

Donnie let the apartment door slam shut behind him, not even attempting to dull the crashing sound it made, and jogged down the hall.

"God Almighty," he grumbled to himself as he smacked his broad palm against the heavy fire door that led to the back stairwell, pushing it open so hard that it cracked against the wall. "Villi *said* he'd taken care of this. If the neighbors complain again, I am giving them *his* fucking cell phone number! Let them wake *his* ass up."

The fire alarm panel had been located on the ground floor on the west side of the building, near one of the service entrances. The idea was that it would be convenient for fire crews in the event of an actual emergency, and out of the way of guests while The Club was in operation. But if this false-alarm bullshit kept happening, he needed to get a remote control switch or have the damn thing relocated to his apartment.

He didn't care how much he owed Blake and The Club; he was *not* paid enough to leave his Grace tied up in his bed, her ass buck-naked and striped red from his belt, while her eyes begged him to come back and make love to her again.

Christ, fucking his woman was a revelation, every single time. Sex and dominance were nothing new to him, but sex with *Grace* was something special. There was a connection between them that went beyond the simple give and take of pleasure and desire. Dominating Grace didn't simply satisfy his need for control; instead, he recognized that he was meeting *her* need to have a strong person to lead her. And he could see, from looking in her eyes, that her choice to submit to him wasn't simply because she wanted to give over control, but because she wanted to meet his need for dominance. It was selflessness, purer and deeper than he'd ever seen or experienced, and he felt it working a change in him.

He was beginning to look at *himself* in different ways, to simultaneously expect more from himself and to feel like he no longer needed to hide his desires, because Grace was more than up to the challenge of handling him, no matter what fantasies his brain conjured up.

Her words from earlier replayed in his mind. *"I'll do anything you tell me, sir. I'm yours to do with what you will."*

Fuck.

He needed to get back to her. He took the stairs two at a time.

The panel, when he reached it, was lit up like a Christmas tree, and Donnie frowned in concentration, trying to remember everything that Villi had told him. Nothing looked like the error displays they'd discussed, goddamn it!

He reached into his back pocket for his cell phone, ready to wake Villi and get to the bottom of this, only to realize he'd left his cell phone on his nightstand.

"*Shit*! Okay, all right... Error code, error code..." he muttered under his breath. He ran his finger across the display, which Villi had told him would flash with the location of the malfunctioning sensor, but the small window which should have shown a location now read, "Dispatch notified."

A tremor of unease snaked up his spine, and he felt goose bumps form on his naked chest.

The dispatch had *not* been contacted, because Villi had disconnected that part of the malfunctioning system to prevent yet another false-alarm callout to their friends at the local fire station. But the computer system was *trying* to alert the fire department, because...

Because both the smoke and heat detectors near the second floor staircase had tripped.

Not just one sensor, but two? Not an error code, but heat *and* smoke detected? He shook his head once, in instinctive denial, but the display didn't change. Understanding settled like lead in his belly, followed by a thrill of fear unlike anything he'd ever encountered. Was it his imagination, or could he smell... smoke?

Holy shit. Grace was up there.

Tied to the bed!

His legs were pounding back up the stairs, bare feet slapping the treads, before his brain had finished articulating the thought. He panted as he reached the third floor, already shouting Grace's name as he tugged the door handle... But it wouldn't budge.

What the hell?

"Grace!" He pulled with both hands, even bracing his foot against the wall beside the door for added leverage, but the magnetic locks that were supposed to fasten the door shut to prevent the spread of fire had somehow engaged.

He beat at the door uselessly with his palm, the metallic clang ringing above the shrill sound of the alarm. She was so close, but he couldn't get to her. *Fuck!*

He flew back down the stairs to the second floor, and that door mercifully clicked open as soon as he tugged on it. He threw it open and pelted down the hall towards the main staircase at the center of the building.

Smoke, heavy and thick, stung his eyes and filled his throat. He took a deep breath of the relatively clean air in the hallway before battling forward again. The noxious fumes were unreal, far worse than he'd ever imagined, and he felt his lungs seize and burn from the chemicals. He moved forward at a crouch, trying to peer through the roiling black haze, only to come up against a wall of flames when he reached the center landing. The stairway to the second floor was impassable and… *holy shit*. The entire office was in flames.

No way to call for help.

The smoke forced him to his knees and he retched. As he crouched there, a decorative brocade panel that draped from the ceiling caught fire and sailed to the ground in a shower of sparks. Several burning embers carried on the drift of smoke to land on his naked chest, and he slapped at himself, barely feeling the burns.

Above the roar of the flames and the alarm, he imagined he could hear Grace calling his name. He forced himself to crawl back in the direction he'd come.

The smoke filled nearly the entire hallway now, and this time when he opened the fire door he did so carefully, closing it behind him as fast as he could to keep the air in the stairway as clear as possible. Then he dropped to his knees once more, coughing black soot from his lungs while tears streamed from his burning eyes and rolled down his face.

Shit. How had the fire gotten so bad so fast? How the hell could he get to Grace?

With a start, he remembered the fire escape on the rear of the building.

He reached out a hand and pulled himself up using the railing, then stumbled down the stairs, past the blinking panel, and out the service entrance into the freezing cold night.

He sucked in the bracing, clear air, even though it made him cough even harder, and considered his next step.

The fire escape ran in a zigzag pattern from the center of the second floor of the building up to his bedroom window on the third floor, with a small landing halfway along. He just needed to get to the second floor.

Donnie ran to the corner of the parking lot where the construction guys kept their equipment and nearly sighed in relief as he spied what he'd been looking for. He grabbed an aluminum ladder maybe twelve feet tall from the back corner, where it had apparently been abandoned by one of the masonry companies that had come earlier in the spring. He hauled it out without a thought to the loud crash of the discarded wood and other supplies in the pile as they resettled.

An annoyed voice from the spa building across the alley called, "Is that the damn alarm again?"

"Call 911!" Donnie screamed, his voice hoarse and thready. "It's a fire!"

"No way! A real fire?" the voice demanded. "Are you kidding?"

But Donnie wasn't sticking around to chat. "Fucking *now*. My *girl* is in there!"

His girl. His future. His Grace. His whole damn *world*.

He hauled the ladder across the parking lot and propped it

against the building where it looked like it would be just long enough to get him to the fire escape. *Thank Christ.* The fucking thing shook like a leaf in a breeze as soon as he was halfway up, and he took a precious second to steady himself, reaching through the rungs to touch the rough brick of the building. Up and up he climbed, trying not to focus on the shaking, or the fall that he was likely to take, or whether the stonemasons had left the ladder behind on *purpose* because the fucking thing was missing one of its stabilizing feet. *Grace*, he thought. Gotta get to Grace.

Finally, *finally*, he got to the top and reached up, ready to grab the fire escape ladder, only to find that it was still two feet above him.

No!

The alarm was still blaring shrilly, and although no flames or smoke were yet visible from outside the building, he imagined he could hear the roar of them as they climbed inexorably closer to the third floor, creeping down the hall to his apartment. Without planning, without even considering the consequences, he jumped…

And caught the ladder extension on the bottom rung.

He held on as tight as he could as the extension descended, then climbed back up until he was firmly on the black metal staircase. He flew up the stairs, mentally assessing the strength of the glass on the window in his bedroom, and whether he had time to shuck his jeans and wrap them around his foot to provide a small measure of protection before he broke it, when the sight inside his bedroom had him stopping and flattening himself against the side of the building.

Grace wasn't alone in the room.

A figure dressed in black stood with their back to the window, pointing a gun at Grace with one shaking hand.

Panic seized him, bringing the choking red haze to cloud his vision. How had Mikey found her? Had Joe given them away? Donnie vowed then and there to end his brother if he'd had one fucking thing to do with harming Grace. Fuck brotherhood. Fuck family.

Grace was all that mattered.

But then a single beam of logic cut through the haze.

Mikey wanted her, *needed* her, for Salazar. Why would he set fire to the building while she was still inside it? Or, *fuck*, why wouldn't he be freeing her right now, and forcing her down the stairs?

Donnie peered around the window for one more glimpse, just as the figure in black slipped off their hood… and shook out her long brown hair.

Holy fucking hell.

Julie?

He'd suspected that something was off with her, but never *this*.

He sank back against the wall, and willed back the blind panic that had driven him up to this point. He sucked in a deep breath and forced himself *not* to think of the terrified expression on Grace's face, nor the fire that was no doubt racing across the floor towards his apartment. He instinctively knew that if he broke the window and charged to the rescue, Julie would lash out. He needed to handle this with finesse… with *control*. He needed to formulate a plan.

Please, God.

He glanced up and saw exactly the sign from Heaven he'd needed.

Further back along the fire escape, the window to the bathroom was open, just a crack. No doubt Gracie had opened it earlier yesterday, when the weather had been mild, and forgotten to close and lock it. On any other day, he would have very firmly pointed out the inherent safety risk, and reddened her ass enough to ensure that she never made *that* error again.

Tonight, he felt like singing Alleluia.

He climbed onto the railing of the staircase, and was just able to get his hands on the window casing enough to pry it up, inch by careful inch. When the opening was as wide as he could make it reaching from this awkward angle, he held his breath and reached up with both hands, grasping the windowsill and pulling himself up and over until his forearms were inside, and the rest of his body dangled against the side of the building.

And then a loud voice from the other room rose above the whine of the fire alarm, and what he heard chilled him to the bone.

"Who the fuck do you think you are?"

It was Julie, but *not*. Gone was the strange, breathy, high-pitched voice she'd always used with Donnie. Her voice now was hard and filled with pain as she threatened Grace.

Donnie's bare feet scrabbled against the rough exterior of the building, needing just the tiniest bit more traction so that he could lever himself up. His toes dug in and he pushed, wriggling through the narrow opening as silently as he could, first his head… then his shoulders.

"I tried to be nice to you, Grace. I tried to tell you the other day in the parking lot that guys like Donnie have the girls they fuck and the girls they fall in love with. Remember?" A pause, and then more harshly, "*I said 'Remember?'*"

Grace's tear-filled voice stuttered out a reply. "Y-yes. I remember!"

"But you didn't stay away!" Julie accused. "You let him fuck you anyway, didn't you?"

"I-I thought you meant that I..." Grace's voice trailed off.

"You thought I meant... *what*? That *you* were the girl Donnie would fall in *love* with?" Julie cackled, her laughter glee-filled and absolutely insane. A wave of terror threatened to swamp him and he wriggled faster, nearly dislocating his shoulder in his haste. The bathroom window opened into the tub, and the tiled walls provided nothing for him to grip onto.

"Oh, you're so sweet, Grace. So silly. How could you ever think a *man* like Donnie could love a *girl* like you? Oh, he'll fuck you," the bitch allowed in a sing-song voice. "He might even play cute little tie-down games like this with you. But you will never understand what makes him tick. You will never get off on the pain like I do!"

"I get off on making *him* get off," Grace retorted quietly. And though a corner of his brain roared in pride at her bravery, the remainder of him vowed to tan her ass again the second she was free. Why the hell was she arguing?

Julie didn't seem to understand either. The sound of flesh slapping against flesh rang out like a gunshot, even over the wail of the alarm. Grace cried out, and Donnie froze as fresh fury flooded him. Heedless of the pain, he forced his hips to shimmy through the window, catching himself with his hands against the bottom of the tub.

"You don't know the first fucking *thing* about getting him off!" Julie cried. "How long have you known him, little girl? Ten minutes?"

Grace wisely kept her mouth shut, and didn't correct Julie's assumption. Despite his precarious position, Donnie heaved a sigh of relief.

"I've been there for him for months!" Julie continued. "I've made myself *indispensable* around this place. I know how to work the alarms and all the electrical systems, I know how to trigger the magnets on the fire doors, and I know where the painters keep all of their supplies. The members love me, the staff loves me, and Donnie loves me too! Oh, he tried to deny it. Told me he wanted to stay professional, because that's just the kind of honorable guy he is… or *was* until you came along." Julie's voice descended into bitterness. "But I could see through it. He chose *me* for all his demonstrations because he knew I craved the same things he does."

Donnie carefully pulled his legs through the window, one after the other, setting his feet soundlessly on the bottom of the tub.

"Once *you* were here, he tried to keep away from me. But I knew we were destined to be together all along. I knew he just needed me to *show him* how good it could be between us. That's why I made sure Carly got sick the day she was scheduled to do the demo. And sure enough, once he had my ass splayed out on that spanking bench, Donnie couldn't hold back. I have *never* had someone take me to the places he's taken me!" Her voice quivered with remembered longing, and Donnie felt his stomach turn.

Certifiable! Had the woman really lit the place on fire? For fuck's sake, why?

"S-so, what? You're going to *shoot* me, just to get me out of the way so that you can be with Donnie?" Grace demanded.

Julie snorted. "You sound so traumatized, precious. Next you'll be telling me you thought you and I were friends." She laughed again, but then grew serious. Her voice was quiet, and Donnie strained to hear it over the shrill alarm. "I didn't *want* it to have to come to this, you know. If you'd left when I talked to you... If Carter had managed to take you this morning, like I paid him to—"

"You paid the man who grabbed me?" Grace was outraged. "Outside the coffee shop?"

Julie snorted again. "Yes. I'd been following you two all morning, and I took my shot the minute you stepped away from him. But my idiot cousin was no match for Donnie. God, did you like the show my Donnie gave you?" Julie's voice rose in excitement. "The way he lost control? *That's* the kind of man Donnie is. He shouldn't have to keep himself in check the way he does with you. He shouldn't have to hide. With *me*, he won't!"

"H-he's going to be back any minute!" Grace warned her desperately. "He just went to shut off the alarm and he'll be back! He's never gonna be with you if he knows what you've done."

His hands and feet were cut to shit from scrabbling against the brick outside, his lungs still burned from exertion and the lingering effects of the smoke, and his legs could barely support him, but he pushed himself up from his crouch and stood. He braced a hand against the tile, steadying himself as his head swam.

"Oh, sweetie," Julie crooned. "I almost, *almost*, feel bad. Hurting you is gonna be like hurting a sweet, little puppy! I really do think I'll be *traumatized.*" She gave an unconvincing sob that turned to laughter. "Or I'll play it off that way, anyhow. Once they find your remains in the wreckage, and Donnie's precious club is gone, he and I will have to lean on each other more than ever! He'll be all sad and mopey because he's lost his club *and* his little fuck toy, and I... well, I'll be as *indispensable* to him as I always am!"

"W-what do you mean *wreckage?*" Grace's voice wobbled.

Julie giggled. "I *mean*, I lit a tiny little fire on the second floor. Can you smell the smoke? Fire for purity, you know? Burn it all down, and start new. That's the way."

Where *was* the fire department? *Fuck.*

God, he needed to get in there.

"You set fire to the building? With Donnie inside?" Donnie shut his eyes as Grace's words flowed through him. Crazy-scared as she was, her first thought had still been for him.

"No, silly!" Julie argued. "I locked Donnie *out*. Secured all the fire doors so he can't get up here and cut the landlines in the office so he can't call out, even if he manages to get to the office somehow."

"B-but that means you're stuck up here, too!" Grace reminded her. "If you untie me... If you call the fire department right now? I'll go, Julie. I'll leave town, I swear I will. I'll walk away and you'll never see me again. I promise!"

Donnie tiptoed across the bathroom floor and paused in the open door to the hallway. The smoke was beginning to seep beneath the apartment door now, and he knew they had only minutes left to escape. He thought he heard the noise of sirens in the distance and prayed that the firefighters would get there in time.

He turned towards the bedroom in time to see Julie smile widely and lean down to stroke Grace's face with the barrel of the gun.

"So, so sweet. You know, I can almost understand what he sees in you!" she mused. "No, honey, you see, I also know how to *release* the magnets on the fire door. I'll stumble out the back exit into Donnie's waiting arms, just grateful to be alive, and no one will suspect a thing. You're the last loose end I need to tie up, Grace." She stood back and aimed the gun.

Instinct, overwhelming and unstoppable, had Donnie stepping through the door and into the room, dragging Julie's attention—and the focus of her gun—away from Grace.

"Donnie!" Julie cried in confusion, her eyes pinging back and forth from him to the bed. "Donnie… it's not what it looks like!"

Donnie took one look at Grace, who was still naked on the mattress, covered only by a sheet. He could see that she had twisted one hand loose from the t-shirt that bound her to the bed, and he was confident that she could get the other one loose, too, as soon as Julie was distracted. He gave Grace a small nod when Julie's gaze swung in Grace's direction.

He let his face settle in a sneer as he regarded Grace, and made sure Julie saw it. Then he drawled, "Oh, I think it's pretty obvious what happened here… *sweetheart.*"

He turned his gaze to Julie and looked at her adoringly. Her face scrunched into a frown as she attempted to process his loving look and his tender words.

"You caught this *bitch* trying to sabotage The Club," Donnie said with a smile. "God, I can't believe I was so wrong about her, Julie. Thank God you were here."

From the window, Donnie could see the flashing red and blue lights of the emergency vehicles, but Julie didn't seem to notice. She licked her lips and watched Donnie avidly, her corners of her lips tipping up in a mad little smile. "Y-yes. Yes! I was here tonight doing the…"

"Stockroom inventory?" Donnie supplied, taking a step closer. From the corner of his eye, he could see Grace working her second hand free.

"Yes! Yes, the stockroom. And I saw *her* downstairs setting fires!" Julie accused.

Donnie widened his eyes as though this were news to him. As though he hadn't just had to scale the outside of the building to get here. As though the smoke wasn't, even now, seeping under the apartment door and slithering along the hallway. As though someone other than *Donnie himself* could have tied Grace to his bed.

God. The woman was truly lost to madness. He felt a flash of pity, but ruthlessly quashed it. *Grace* was his only priority. Julie's delusions were something he'd have to use to his advantage.

He took a step towards Julie, eyes wide and concerned.

"Oh, Julie, sweetheart, that's terrible! Are you okay? Did she hurt you?" He pasted a sympathetic look on his face and took another step closer to her.

Julie didn't seem to know what to do with the gun. She swung it back and forth from him to Grace, unable to think clearly. She obviously wanted him closer, but she wasn't sure she could trust him. He needed to push a little harder.

"Whoa! Sweetie, put that down right now!" He made his voice go stern and dominant, just as she would expect, but he let his eyes narrow and his gaze focus on her lips. "I just wanted to make sure you were all right, and give you a kiss!"

"A k-kiss?" Julie whispered, her eyes enormous. "You've never kissed me before!"

"That was *before*, when things were different and I thought I needed to keep my distance. Now I see how clearly we were meant to be together," he told her.

Julie let the gun hang limply at her side as he approached the last few steps. He lifted one hand to cup her cheek, distracting her, while the other hand clamped around the wrist holding the gun. He squeezed her wrist slightly as he lowered his head to hers, and took the gun from her limp hand just before their lips touched.

Yes.

The hand he'd placed on Julie's face moved back further to grab her by the hair, and he forced the woman face-down to the ground before she had a chance to blink. Tucking the gun into his waistband, he grabbed Julie's arms and pinned them behind her, holding her down with his knee to her lower back.

She wriggled against him for a moment, fighting his hold, but the reality of the situation must have finally penetrated the fantasy she'd woven. Her struggles turned to quiet sobs, and Donnie was finally, *finally* able to turn his attention to the woman on the bed.

"Up and dress, Grace!" he barked.

Grace had managed to untangle herself from the shirt, and as he watched, she threw back the sheet and reached for the clothes she'd discarded earlier. She looked supremely pissed off, but otherwise uninjured... and then he noticed that one of her cheeks was red, likely from where Julie had slapped her. He found himself applying just a tiny bit more pressure to Julie's wrists in response. Crazy as Julie might be, he had zero fucking sympathy for anyone who laid a hand on his angel.

"You're all right? Your cheek?" he rasped when Grace had shoved her feet into her shoes and raised her eyes to him.

Grace nodded, but as her eyes raked over his body, her angry expression crumpled and her eyes filled with tears. She took a step toward him as if she couldn't help herself. "Oh my God, Donnie! Your poor chest is burned! And your feet!"

Donnie shook his head, cutting her off. "Not now, angel. Open the window and yell out to let them know we're here. And tell them we have a mentally unstable woman in here who confessed to arson and attempted murder."

She did as he commanded, and seconds later, the rescue squad was hoisting a crane to the window, so Grace wouldn't have to jump from the fire escape.

The smoke was rolling thicker now, filling the room as the flames no doubt engulfed the hall outside. Still, as the firefighter's face appeared outside the window and he held out a hand for Grace, she paused, turned to Donnie, and somehow, impossibly, found it in her to smile.

"Love you, Donnie," she said, as she stepped over the windowsill.

Again, he marveled at his woman's strength, but for once in his life, he also had to wonder at his own dumb luck. The building he'd designed and helped renovate was burning down around him, his future was uncertain, and he had no idea how he would get Grace free of Mikey and Salazar, but at that moment he couldn't find it in himself to be anything but thankful. He knew how to build a life from the ground up. God knew, he'd done it before. He could do it again. As long as Grace was safe and happy and *by his side*, he had everything he needed.

"Brother, you are not gonna believe the phone call I just got."

Donnie glanced up from his sprawl on the couch in Slay and Alice's comfortable family room and regarded Slay with eyes that still burned from the smoke. Despite showers he'd taken, first at the hospital and then again when they'd arrived at Slay's house, Donnie was pretty sure he was gonna smell, and *feel*, like barbecue for the next few days.

"Slay, if there were ever a time to get me to believe the unbelievable? It's right fucking now," Donnie grumbled and his right arm, which held his sleeping woman firmly at his side, tightened around her involuntarily. Some of the shock seemed to have worn off, and as it had, Donnie's anger had returned. He couldn't *believe* all that the devastation Julie had wrought through her delusions, and it turned his stomach to think how close he'd come to losing Grace forever. Still, he told Slay, "Lay it on me."

But Slay didn't answer right away. He handed Donnie a mug of coffee and perched himself on the coffee table next to Donnie's bandaged feet. "You doing okay?" he asked.

Donnie snorted softly, not wanting to wake Grace. "Yeah, Marine. I've got two broken toes, a couple tiny burns, and the skin on my hands and feet are torn to hell, but it ain't fatal. I'll live."

Slay nodded, but when still he didn't continue, Donnie prompted. "So? The phone call?"

"It'll keep for a minute. Drink first." Slay lifted his chin in the direction of Donnie's coffee cup.

Donnie rolled his eyes. "Jesus. Give a man a couple of kids and suddenly he tries to parent every-fucking-body?" he grumbled.

"Fuck you, Don!" Slay snapped. "Just... give me a damn minute to be glad you're okay, yeah? I get a call from the QPD in the middle of the night that our building is a total fucking loss, and *oh yeah*, one of our employees was a psychotic bitch from hell who lit the place on fire after *oh right*, attempting to murder my friend's woman, and *just for kicks*, that friend was taken by ambulance to the goddamn hospital for smoke inhalation and broken bones because he had to *scale the side of the burning building* like he's some fucking Irish-Surfer-Boy-Spiderman with a death wish!" A vein in Slay's forehead throbbed by the time he finished speaking.

Donnie blinked. He wasn't sure he could remember ever seeing Slay this worked up about something that wasn't a Patriots playoff game or Chalo Salazar, but *damn*. He bit back a smile, then raised the mug to his lips and took a sip. "Real good coffee," he told Slay mildly.

Slay snorted and shook his head. "Asshole," he replied affectionately.

"Seriously, though," Donnie continued. "You hear anything from the fire inspector yet? Is the building…"

Slay shook his head. "Way too early for that shit, bud." He tipped his head towards the large French doors that led to the backyard, and Donnie could see that the sky was still orange-and-pink tinged with sunrise. "They need to get inspectors on the scene in daylight to really see anything, and the official report won't come back for a few *days*. But unofficially, there's nothing we didn't expect. Julie knew where the painters kept their paint thinner and she spread it all over the center lobby on the second floor, as well as the office and the staircase. By her own admission, she'd been monkeying with the sensors all along. She flirted with Villi's freckle-faced little assistant, Gil…"

"Gib," Donnie corrected, and Slay nodded.

"Right, Gib. She flirted with the kid, who probably thought he'd won the damn lottery, and he explained all the inner workings of the system to her. She wanted you good and pissed off by the system malfunction, so that she could swoop in and save the day and get your attention." Slay shook his head in disgust.

"Yeah? Well, she's got my fucking attention now," Donnie spat, his teeth locked together and his hand clenching around the handle of the coffee mug.

"No shit," Slay agreed darkly. "But then Grace came along, and Julie felt she needed more than just a distraction, she needed to get Grace out of the picture entirely. When Andy mentioned to her that Villi had disconnected the alarm from the central terminal, and it wouldn't alert dispatch… she decided the time was right to make her move. She figured you'd go down to reset the alarm, so she locked you out of the floor. Then she went for Grace."

Donnie blew out a breath and tried to calm himself. Anger right now would do nothing. There was still so much more to be settled, so much more he needed to do to protect Grace.

"Listen," he told Slay. "I appreciate you letting us stay here last night, to get our feet under us. But the last thing I wanna do is bring trouble to your door. *More* trouble besides Julie," he amended. "Salazar was scheduled to be released yesterday from prison. That means his homecoming party is tonight. Clock's run out, man. They'll know within the next few hours that Grace is gone, if they haven't figured it out already. And since we haven't come up with a plan to solve that problem, the safest thing for us to do is get out of town. Just for a while."

He winced as he looked down at Grace. He knew how important it was to her to get free of Mikey for good, so she wouldn't have to constantly be looking over her shoulder and waiting for the other shoe to drop. He would never give up until he'd done exactly that, but he would make sure the woman understood that her well-being was his first priority. He would get her safe and *then* he'd finish up with Mikey.

Slay frowned. "Okay, hold up. First off, *you* didn't bring Julie to our door, Don. I talked to Andy this morning, and he says you were the only one who saw through Julie's act. He says he's sorry he ever doubted you."

Donnie snorted, remembering Andy's defense of Julie and Donnie's instinctive mistrust of the woman.

"And second of all, why don't you wait a couple of hours before you make any plans for getting out of town," Slay said mysteriously. "I got some news this morning that... well. Just table this decision for now, yeah?"

Donnie narrowed his eyes. "Spill."

"Nope." Slay folded his arms over his chest, and his eyes twinkled.

"Slay."

"Donnie?"

"Fucking *talk*, Slater!"

Slay bit his lip and pretended to flip his nonexistent hair. "Oh, Master Nolan," he trilled, falsetto. "Order me around some more! You're so hot when you get all dominant."

Despite himself, Donnie snorted. "*Jesus*."

Slay smiled. "Spoiler: Blake, Elena, Dom, Heidi, Matteo, Hillie, Paul, and Diego are all on their way over."

Donnie felt his mouth drop open. "*All* of them? On a work morning?"

Slay nodded. "Family emergency."

There it was again. *Family*. He'd worried, at one point, that he had nothing to offer Grace. That the various pieces of his soul: the shitty father who'd raised him, the psychotic cousin who'd molded him, the sadistic fantasies that spurred him, the nomadic adventures he craved, made him too damaged for a woman like Grace. But he'd forgotten this incredible family that he'd become a part of.

"What, Tony and Tess were busy?" Donnie joked weakly.

"Nope. They, along with John, had to stop at *Cara* first for supplies. The way things are going, the fucking zombie apocalypse might strike tomorrow, and we don't wanna be low on tiramisu, do we? Especially not with a pregnant Tess on our hands." Slay winked and stood. "Get some rest, bro. Hold your woman. Allie and I are keeping the kids on the other side of the house, so no one will bother you. I'm gonna make breakfast and get the boys off to school, then we'll talk more when everyone gets here."

A few seconds later, Donnie poked the unnaturally still woman at his side.

"Hey!"

"How long have you been pretending to sleep?" he demanded.

"How do you know I was pretending? I was *resting*," she argued. She pushed up carefully, avoiding the burns, and her big brown eyes met his. She looked tired still, but calm. Not remotely afraid, despite what she might have overheard.

"How long?" he repeated, tickling her ribs until she squirmed against him.

"Erm… Somewhere before *Irish-Surfer-Boy-Spiderman*?" she giggled.

"So you heard what I said about leaving town."

He hadn't phrased it as a question, but Grace answered anyway, biting her lip and confirming with a nod. "I did. If that's the way it has to be, Donnie, I'm okay with it."

His head shifted against the back of the sofa to look at her more fully. "Before, you didn't want to live looking over your shoulder," he reminded her.

She ducked her head, pressing a soft kiss to his chest over the worn cotton t-shirt Slay had lent him. "That was *before*," she whispered. "Before, when I was still the princess in the tower, and freedom was the most important thing to me. Before I really understood what it meant to live. Before… you. Now, I don't care where we go, as long as we're together."

Donnie leaned forward and pressed his lips to hers in a chaste kiss. A promise. But Grace opened her lips beneath his and wrapped her hand around his neck, pulling herself closer. The soft, delicious scent of her—spice and sweetness, rich and honest—enveloped him, and he gave himself over to it. He set his coffee cup down on the end table, and wove both of his ruined hands through the soft strands of her hair, pulling her up and over to straddle him. His thumbs cradled her jaw, angling her so that his tongue slid more firmly against hers.

It wasn't until he was hard and aching, until her breath was coming in short little huffs that drove him crazy, that he remembered where they were. A clink of china from the kitchen penetrated his brain and he eased Grace back slowly until she was sitting next to him once more.

"Wrong time and place, baby," he told her reluctantly, his hand stroking over her hair to soothe her.

She nodded, but bit her lip. "Later, then? I really need you, Donnie. I need to feel connected to you." She shook her head in frustration. "I'm not explaining it right."

"I know exactly what you mean. After all that happened last night, you need a reminder that you and I are okay, that we're alive, that no matter what happens, we will always come through it together. I need that, too," he confessed. And there were other needs, as well. The need to mark her again, to claim her, to remind himself that anyone who wanted to harm her would have to go through *him* first. "Here's what we're going to do."

"*You* are going to go upstairs, take a shower, and get dressed in the clothes Allie said you could borrow. Then we're going to meet with everyone and let Elena fuss over us because she can't fucking help herself. We're going to make a plan for the short-term that will keep you safe. And we are absolutely going to make a plan for the long-term, too, because making sure that you are free to live life on your own terms is non-negotiable, Grace. And then, once all that shit is sorted?" His voice dropped to a deep rumble as desire thrummed through him. "Then I am going to find a place where we can be alone, and I am going to remind you who owns every inch of that body."

She shivered, then sucked in a deep breath and stood. But before she left the room, she leaned down and pressed another gentle kiss to his lips.

"Order me around some more!" she teased, quoting Slay's words from earlier.

In an instant, she was over his lap, face-down, laughing as he delivered three stinging slaps to her pajama-clad rear end.

"Anything else to say, Miss Diaz?" he asked as he let her up.

"Just that Slay's right, baby," she told him, her eyes glowing with love and mischief. She pitched her voice high and cooed, "You really *are* hot when you get all dominant!"

She scurried away before he could catch her again thanks to the stupid bandages on his feet, but that was fine. He had plenty of time to teach her a lesson about teasing her man.

An hour later, everyone seemed to arrive simultaneously. Grace had finished her shower, her damp hair was twisted up into a bun, and she looked fresh and clean in a pretty sundress that Alice had given her.

"Keep it," Allie had told Grace with a wink at her husband, as the two women had sliced berries for fruit salad while Donnie and Slay sat at the kitchen island and supervised. "I doubt I'll be able to wear it much before it's out of style."

Grace had seemed confused, but the way Slay preened at the news, Donnie guessed that there would be another Slater baby joining Charlie, Lex, Mason, and Slay in keeping Allie on her toes. Donnie grinned as he stole a berry from Grace's bowl.

Elena *did* fuss over him, as expected, needing to ascertain for herself that his feet were properly bandaged, that he would keep his weight off his injured foot, and that he would wear a walking boot for the rest of the week as the doctor had suggested. Donnie assured her that he would, and then he and Blake exchanged a look of commiseration over her head that said Blake, at least, recognized that the boot would *not* be coming with Donnie when he left Slay's house.

Heidi, Grace, and Hillary helped Tony, Tess, and John organize food in the kitchen, while Dom and Paul took seats on the couches opposite Donnie and continued an argument they'd apparently been having on the way in.

"Don't get me wrong, Heidi and I love the place," Dom was saying. "The baby loves it. Hell, even the dog loves it. But it's a money pit. We try to get up there every weekend in the summer, but it's tough to keep up the repairs."

"You talking about your cabin up in the boondocks?" Donnie interjected.

Dom nodded. "You looking for a property? I can rent you one cheap," he joked.

"I still say you should've gone South," Paul told Dom. "Cape Cod's closer to Boston, and I'll take the beach over the woods any day. Plus, you'd have no trouble renting it out in the off season."

"Yeah, but you know how Heidi feels about Maine," Dom

said, his voice softening as he spoke of his wife. "The cabin's not just a financial investment, it's an emotional one."

The doorbell rang and Allie passed through the room to answer it, while everyone else piled in from the kitchen and claimed their seats on the sofas and the plush area rug.

Paul shook his head, bringing his knee up at an angle to sit sideways facing Dom with his elbow against the back of the sofa. "You know, Heids," Paul told his best friend and business partner as she perched on the arm of the sofa next to Dom. "I wish I could tape this conversation and go back in time a few years, back to when you were absolutely panicked about getting involved with this guy, wondering if you could trust him and whether you could make it work."

Heidi laughed softly and leaned against Dom. "Nah. Wouldn't have helped. I had to go through all the confusion and craziness to get to where we are."

Grace reclaimed her seat next to Donnie, cuddling up against his side. "You think that will be us, a few years down the line?" she whispered.

Donnie shook his head. "Nah." He smirked when he saw her annoyed frown and tugged a lock of her pretty dark hair. "That's us *now*, honey. You and me... we know each other inside and out. We already know we can trust each other. We already know we're gonna work."

She smiled, but then she looked beyond Donnie's shoulder. Her smile fell and tension gripped her small frame.

"Pedro?" she asked, her eyes wide with surprise.

Donnie turned his head to face the trio of men who trailed Allie back to the family room. Matteo gave him a chin lift before seating himself next to Hillary on the floor, but Donnie barely acknowledged him, his attention focused on the other two men; Pedro, who looked a thousand times better than the last time Donnie saw him, and Diego Santiago, who looked a thousand times worse.

"*Ah, Dios.* Thank God you're okay, Gracia Maria," Pedro breathed, saying Grace's name in Spanish, the way their parents used to. "I was so worried!"

The worst of Pedro's visible wounds were all but healed now, though the bruising on his face would likely remain for some time. His hair was neatly combed, and his eyes had lost their hunted look. He seemed rested, almost *cheerful.*

Donnie felt his temper spike as he took in Pedro's demeanor. Did the asshole have no clue what the past week had been like for his sister? He didn't look particularly worried.

Diego shoved Pedro from behind, forcing him into a straight-backed chair near the fireplace. "*Caillate, cabrón!*" he spat. "Nobody wants to hear a word out of your mouth. Your sister wouldn't have been in trouble at all if not for you!"

Diego looked absolutely exhausted. His skin had a sickly pallor, and his eyes were bloodshot and sunken, like he hadn't slept for days. His voice was thick, as though each word required effort to push past his lips, and he looked *lost.*

"Pedro, what the fuck are you doing back in town?" Donnie demanded. "You don't think we have enough to worry about right now?"

Pedro scowled. "I didn't bring *myself*, Don. I…"

"I brought him," Diego sighed, sinking into another straight-backed chair. "Took him from Lucas's safe house this morning. After last night… hiding don't matter anymore."

Alice, who had disappeared for a moment, came back carrying a mug of coffee, which Diego accepted with a grateful smile. He blew out a breath.

"You all know I've been, uh... an associate of Chalo Salazar," Diego said, with a sideways look at Pedro.

Pedro nodded, seeming to accept this at face value. Clearly he'd had dealings with Diego in the past and known him in that capacity. Donnie sighed, wondering if he would have accepted Diego's cover so easily if he'd still been on Mikey's payroll. Everyone else in the room nodded, but remained silent, understanding that Diego didn't want to share the undercover nature of his association with Chalo.

"Chalo Salazar was released from prison yesterday morning at eleven-fifteen," Diego said. And although they had all been well aware that it would happen, he felt a new tension settle over the room. Even Pedro looked worried.

Then Diego continued, "And he was shot to death at seven-thirty yesterday evening."

"Shot!" Allie said, looking to Slay for confirmation. Slay nodded at her, then looked at Donnie and nodded again. *This* was the information that would change Donnie's plans to leave town.

Everyone else seemed stunned, too shocked to speak or even to move.

Jesus Christ. After everything the asshole had done... dead? It didn't seem possible. And, Donnie acknowledged to himself, it didn't seem *fair*. He wanted justice, for God's sake. He'd wanted that bastard to pay a thousand times over for the harm that he'd caused to their little family.

"How?" Donnie demanded finally. "Who?"

Diego shrugged. "Double tap to the head. Professional looking. As for who... best guess is *El Jefe*, whoever the fuck he is. I don't know. I just... don't know." He closed his eyes and shook his head, and Donnie wondered what images were playing behind his closed eyelids.

"In the past three weeks, each of Chalo's lieutenants have been eliminated one by one. It started with Hector Montero, but they got to Osbaldo Nunez, Cas Reyes, and just a couple of hours ago, Joachim Calder. That's it. They're all gone." His voice was bleak and heavy, and Donnie realized that despite the fact that the men Diego named had been Chalo Salazar's lieutenants, they'd also been Diego's daily companions for the past several *years*. However complicated Diego's feelings about them had been in life, it was clear that some part of him grieved them in death.

Pedro sucked in a breath, staring at Diego appraisingly, but Diego paid no attention. His eyes sought and held Donnie's. "Don…" he said solemnly. "They got to Mikey, too."

Oh.

Now it was Donnie's turn to close his eyes. To inhale deeply. There had been a time, before the blood and the killing, before the drugs and the money and the final exile, that Mikey Nolan had been his savior, plucking Donnie from the squalor of his dad's house and giving him a purpose in life. Now Donnie understood all too well the complicated grief Diego seemed to feel. Donnie had been prepared to eliminate his cousin himself, if it had come down to it, but now, as the weight of the loss settled on his shoulders, he wasn't sure if committing that act would have changed something fundamental within himself.

"Joe?" Donnie demanded, as a new worry occurred to him. "Karen and the kids?"

But Diego shook his head. "Nah, they're fine. God, Don, Joe is small-time, you know? He's not on anybody's radar. Hasn't done anything more serious than pass messages for years."

"Until the part where he helped hold my sister captive," Pedro said, sitting forward angrily. But Diego turned on him.

"Are you serious right now? Joe did what he did because going along with Mikey kept Joe's kids safe! *He* didn't steal three quarters of a million dollars from Mikey. *Jesus.* How have you managed to stay alive all these years when you can't keep your fucking mouth *shut, pendejo?*"

Pedro shrank back in his chair, watching Diego with eyes that were suddenly wide and fearful. "So, what are you going to do now?" he asked in a soft voice.

Diego's jaw hardened and he stared at the wall. "I don't fucking know."

Do? What the hell did Diego have to do? His assignment was over now that Salazar was dead. Donnie shook his head and looked from Matteo to Slay for an explanation. Slay took a breath and shook his head sadly. Whatever Donnie was missing, it wasn't good.

Pedro licked his lips, still watching Diego carefully, as though he were a snake who might turn and strike at any moment. "What does this mean for me? Or for *Grace*, I mean."

Diego snorted. "Yeah. I'm sure that's what you meant. Mikey is dead, so your debt to him is cancelled. But for your own safety, Pedro, leave Boston and don't come back. You hear me? And as for Grace…"

Diego looked up, caught Grace's eyes, and his mouth twisted in a half-hearted smile.

"She's free to do whatever she likes with whomever she likes. And if anyone says differently, they'll answer to me." His voice and eyes grew hard as he looked back at Pedro. "I'm going to make it clear that she, along with everyone in this room apart from *you*, is under my protection."

"Under *your* protection, bro?" Tony laughed. "You setting yourself up an army?"

Diego turned to look at Tony. His eyes were solemn, though his face was expressionless. And as the bottom dropped out of Donnie's stomach, he finally understood.

"He already *has* one," Donnie croaked, sitting forward and grabbing his head with both hands. "Oh, *fuck*, Diego. You're the last one left. The last of Chalo's lieutenants."

The entire room seemed to suck in a shocked breath as the implications of this dropped across their minds one after another, like dominoes. Diego was the last lieutenant, the last trusted member of Chalo's organization. And while Donnie had somehow assumed that Chalo's death would finally set Diego free from the undercover mission that had become his fucking *life*, the opposite was actually true.

If they ever wanted to find the identity of *El Jefe*, if they ever wanted to shut down the sex trafficking operation *El Jefe* was setting up in Boston, Diego needed to maintain his cover…

And become the new leader of Chalo's organization, himself.

"The king is dead," Pedro mocked softly. "Long live the king."

The End

Epilogue

"Oh my God! They even have chocolates on the pillow!"

Grace squealed like a little girl and ran to the balcony of the huge, swanky, luxury suite Slay had managed to secure for them after a few phone calls. She hadn't ever seen anything like it in her life. There was a glass elevator in the very center of the hotel, a waterfall, a legit, bonafide, actual *waterfall* in the lobby, with fancy rocks and places to sit, and she half-expected fairies to flit about, it was that magical. And the *room*. It was honest to God bigger than the apartment she'd grown up in, with a bathroom big enough for a hot tub, a mammoth bed, a kitchenette, and a huge, wrap-around couch nestled in front of a fire place.

"You need a place to chill," Slay had said. "Get your shit together."

And boy did he have some connections. This place was astounding. The balcony overlooked the harbor, azure horizon touching the wharf in downtown Boston, a small table and chairs on the balcony beckoning them to come and sit in quiet. As she stood, her hands on the rail, looking out at the crashing waves, she felt Donnie come up behind her, his powerful presence tangible before he even touched her. He exuded safety, protection...love.

Warm, strong arms wrapped around her from behind, and he cradled her up against his chest. She could smell the leather of the jacket he still wore, but only had a split second to register the scent before she felt his mouth on her cheek, then her neck, trailing kisses along the sensitive, bare skin. "You like chocolates on your pillow, angel?" he whispered in her ear. "I'll put chocolates on your pillow every fucking day if it makes you happy."

She closed her eyes, suddenly overcome with emotion. He must have felt the shift, and turned her around gently to look at him. Placing a hand under her chin, he lifted her eyes, and his own sobered. "Talk to me, Grace." It was a soft command, but she knew now he expected to be obeyed, and though she didn't know quite how to put what she felt into words, she decided she'd give it her best shot.

"It feels so different," she whispered. "It seems I spent my whole life on a balcony that kept me prisoner, away from everything I wanted, locked away like Rapunzel in a tower. You have no idea how I -- I would dream about you climbing that tower and coming to rescue me."

His beautiful brown eyes softened, warming, as he released her chin and pulled her face to his chest, the warmth of his clean black t-shirt flooding her senses. Never had she felt so safe. Never had she felt so *treasured*.

"And now," she continued, her face pressed up against him as a lump rose in her throat. "Up here on *this* balcony? I'm no longer a prisoner. I have you back." Tears stung her eyes and her nose tingled as he held her close. "And when I look out across *this* balcony?" she whispered. "I don't feel apart, and imprisoned, and helpless. I feel like that ocean that reaches out to eternity has endless possibilities. That I can be who I want to be." It was hard to say how she felt but as he held her, the wind at her back and the distant crashing of waves in the background, she knew then what it was. "Donnie, for the first time in my life, I feel *free.*"

His arms tightened around her. "You are, angel. And I'll make sure of that til the day I draw my last breath."

A tear escaped and rolled down her cheek, and she felt the pad of his thumb gently swipe it away. "I know you will," she whispered. He was her hero, and he always would be.

They stood like that in silence, and she had no doubt he was as blown away by the reality of this...the two of them together now, with no one and nothing standing between them...as she was. "I don't think I need anything else," she said, but as he held her, her tummy growled audibly.

He chuckled. "Is that right?" he asked. "Because I think your stomach says otherwise. Come on, honey. Let's get something to eat."

He released her, but took her hand, leading her off the balcony and into the suite. "Where do you want to go?" she asked.

"I've got a place in mind," he said, opening the door, but giving the room one final glance before he gestured her out. "And tonight, we'll make good use of this room."

He winked, smacking her ass as she exited, and just like that, she tingled with anticipation. God, he had her number. She couldn't wait to see what he had in store for her.

Her belly full after a lunch of the most delicious thin crust pizza Boston's North End had to offer, she felt content holding onto Donnie's torso, the bike rumbling beneath them, as they left the city and branched out to a quieter, more secluded spot. He wouldn't tell her where he was taking her.

"You'll see," he hollered over his shoulder. "I've been planning this since you were thirteen years old."

What?

Again, her throat felt too tight, and her nose stung. Would she ever get used to this?

Did she want to?

The noise of the city faded as they traveled further, busy intersections merging to just one narrow strip of paved road that stretched out in front of them. They'd been traveling for a while and though she didn't know where, and she didn't much care, as long as she was with him.

He turned the bike left, down an even narrower road, and as the paved road gave way to hardened dirt, he slowed the bike. They were in a wooded area now, the sun barely peeking through the tops of the trees, the shade making her shiver. He helped her off the bike, and without a word, removed his leather jacket and nestled it over her shoulders, then nabbed her hand, and walked her in silence to a pathway. Tiny clumps of violets and indigo crocuses poked through thick layers of pine needles and dead leaves, and vibrant, spiky green ferns grew along the edges of rocks and tree roots, reminders that even in darkness, hope blooms. Grace's heartbeat accelerated, as she knew they were on the cusp of something special. She'd waited oh-so long, but *he had been worth the wait.*

Sunlight broke through an opening in the trees. She heard the brook before she saw it.

"Oh, Donnie," she whispered. "You remembered."

He released her hand just long enough to take a familiar, yellowed, tattered piece of paper from his wallet. She could see the stream she'd sketched, bordered with wildflowers and pine needles, and the scroll of her teen-aged signature at the very bottom of the page. It looked just like the stream that lay before them now.

"How did you find it?" she whispered.

He shrugged, his eyes filled with pride. "Found it about five years ago. I come out here sometimes, when I need to get away. In my mind, it belongs to you. It was a way I could feel connected even when it was too painful to think about you, but now we get to share it. I knew it was time to show you. It's a special place, for a special day."

A special day?

She looked at him in bewilderment as he dropped to one knee. Could her heart beat faster? Would the tumultuous feelings within her ever settle?

"I love you, Grace Diaz. I'd lay down my life to keep you safe. Now that I have you, I don't ever want to let you go. Marry me?"

"Yes," she said, voice shaking with emotion, as he took both her hands in his, unable to say much more. "Yes," she whispered again.

And as he gathered her in his arms, the trickling of water behind them and flickers of sunlight warming them, they held each other, the promise of what would come as endless as the trailing brook that faded into the horizon. They'd been through hell and back, and come out stronger for it.

There was no ring, and she was glad. She didn't want formalities and ritual. She already had everything she wanted right here in her arms.

THE END

Jane Henry

USA Today bestselling author Jane Henry pens stern but loving alpha heroes, feisty heroines, and emotion-driven happily-ever-afters. She writes what she loves to read: kink with a tender touch. Jane is a hopeless romantic who lives on the East Coast with a houseful of children and her very own Prince Charming.

Don't miss these exciting titles by Jane Henry and Blushing Books!

A Thousand Yesses

Bound to You series
Begin Again, Book 1
Come Back To Me, Book 2
Complete Me, Book 3

Boston Doms Series
By Jane Henry and Maisy Archer
My Dom, Book 1
His Submissive, Book 2
Her Protector, Book 3
His Babygirl, Book 4
His Lady, Book 5
Her Hero, Book 6

My Redemption, Book 7

Anthologies
Hero Undercover
Sunstrokes

Connect with Jane Henry
janehenrywriter.blogspot.com
janehenrywriter@gmail.com

Maisy Archer

Maisy is an unabashed book nerd who has been in love with romance since reading her first Julie Garwood novel at the tender age of 12. After a decade as a technical writer, she finally made the leap into writing fiction several years ago and has never looked back. Like her other great loves - coffee, caramel, beach vacations, yoga pants, and her amazing family - her love of words has only continued to grow... in a manner inversely proportional to her love of exercise, house cleaning, and large social gatherings. She loves to hear from fellow romance lovers, and is always on the hunt for her next great read.

Don't miss these exciting titles by Jane Henry and Maisy Archer with Blushing Books!

Boston Doms Series
By Jane Henry and Maisy Archer
My Dom, Book 1
His Submissive, Book 2
Her Protector, Book 3
His Babygirl, Book 4
His Lady, Book 5
Her Hero, Book 6
My Redemption, Book 7

Anthologies
Hero Undercover
Sunstrokes

Connect with Maisy Archer
janeandmaisy.com

Blushing Books

Blushing Books is one of the oldest eBook publishers on the web. We've been running websites that publish spanking and BDSM related romance and erotica since 1999, and we have been selling eBooks since 2003. We hope you'll check out our hundreds of offerings at http://www.blushingbooks.com.

Blushing Books Newsletter

Please join the Blushing Books newsletter
to receive updates & special promotional offers.
You can also join by using your mobile phone:
Just text BLUSHING to 22828.

CPSIA information can be obtained
at www.ICGtesting.com
Printed in the USA
LVHW011638180520
655945LV00004B/400